NOT DONE YET

DAVID TIENTER

NOT DONE YET
by
David Tienter
Copyright © David Tienter 2014
Edited by: Joann Smith
Cover Illustration Copyright © 2014 by Ravenswood Publishing
Published by Enigma Press
(An Imprint of Ravenswood Publishing)

GMTA Publishing Group, LLC
6296 Philippi Church Rd.
Raeford, NC 28376
http://www.gmtapublishing.com

Printed in the U.S.A.

ISBN-13: 9780692322789
ISBN-10: 0692322787

DEDICATION

I want to thank my wife, Anne, for her support and encouragement. I could not have completed this work without her.

TABLE OF CONTENTS

CHAPTER ONE

I drive now. Driving keeps my mind in limbo, not busy remembering or reflecting, just driving. For me every day now goes slowly faster. Long days filled with mindless driving, restless nights fighting memories in a small tent. As I head further north the campgrounds are emptier. September nights are getting colder and kids have returned to school. I prepare my meals in one pan with opened cans of fruit for dessert. I talk with other campers occasionally usually discussing weather and destinations. I am heading north to South Dakota, with childhood memories of fishing and camping in the Missouri River Valley and its system of dammed-up lakes.

My Jeep contains the remaining memories of a lifetime. My wife, a meticulous computer programmer, forgot one morning that she was cooking breakfast. She was watching television in another room when I smelled the smoke. No damage done, but we felt she should get a medical checkup, just to make sure. A test performed by her doctor revealed a brain anomaly.

The hell of modern medicine reached into every facet of our lives in our attempt to heal up that little anomaly which turned out to be a malignant tumor. She had always been a lithe, magical creature. She was slowly robbed of her body, her beauty, any hope, and finally her dignity. Until her death, she remained steadfast in her faith.

I have always been the average looking guy. I'm taller than most at six foot four and weighing between two hundred and two twenty depending on which holiday has just passed. I always had an easy way with making friends being an average Joe, and for my whole life I have loved the one woman. I have always felt bad for the really handsome guys and the really homely guys as they are the ones who have the most problems in life.

Alone now, I usually stop before dark. I can see well enough to drive at night but it does strain my eyes. At the age of seventy, it can be difficult to go on living alone or to even plan a new start in life. I am not going to begin over; I will just roll within the river of my life as the current gains speed pushing me, always pushing me on. I will try to enjoy my given allotment of time in finding gentle joys.

I camp in a cold deserted campground overlooking Lewis and Clark Lake. It has not been mowed or raked for weeks. Weeds proliferate, and leaves pile up under every wind stop. This site is less than thirty yards wide and forty yards long with six fire rings. Each ring is meant to designate one site. Only tents are allowed, no Class A's or trailers allowed, the one faucet has been turned off for the season, so no running water, no electricity, but there is an outhouse located a short distance down a path. There are four cedar trees strategically placed around the outhouse, perhaps they are meant to be a wind break. Tents here need strong staking because in South Dakota, the wind seems to always blow from the west. The state has not put a lot of funding into these small sites; they mow occasionally and collect the money always. A small post with a collection box gives the rules: fires in fire ring only, police your area, eight dollars per night, no cash only checks. The best part of this site is the view of Lewis and Clark Lake which stretches majestically below the knoll it sits on.

I have erected my tent, started a small fire within the ring, and now I take my fly rod down the grassy path to the lake. Several knee surgeries have made my mobility all-around bad but downhill is the toughest for me. I once saw a lady with an artificial knee slip on grass while walking downhill and her foot ended up trapped beneath her. Her knee bent so far that it broke the implanted prosthesis. Her husband told me later that she had spent three months hospitalized in intensive care while they replaced the artificial knee and fought the staph infection. The lesson to be learned here is walk carefully downhill. It takes almost twenty minutes to navigate the short grassy path downward. I tie a Royal Coachman fly on my tippet and within fifteen minutes bring a fine small walleye in to shore. I fillet it on a small flat rock letting the head and insides float away in the river; turtle food. I rinse my knife, re-sheath it on my hip and returned to camp. Uphill only takes a few minutes and three minutes later that walleye is crackling nicely in my fry pan. I open a can of beans. Tummy full, camp set for the night, I watch the beautiful Dakota skies unfold before me. I feel content and sleepy. Today has been a very good day.

CHAPTER TWO

He is a tall man, six foot one inch, weighing two hundred and forty pounds. He is twenty eight. Proud of his body, he has heavily muscled arms, a deep muscular chest, and powerful legs. He is twenty to thirty pounds overweight and calls it his soft cement. He works at a beef slaughter plant as a lugger carrying the carcasses from cold storage to be hung in the refrigerated eighteen wheelers. His hours of work are very early mornings until just past noon on most days. It's a shift he works with twelve other men. They all must be very strong to do the work. It is seldom anyone talks to him. His work leaves afternoons free for riding and his night open for drinking at CHICKS BAR. No mental abilities needed on his job, he can arrive hung-over and half drunk, no one cares. No one says anything to him anyway. Once he makes full gang member, he will quit this grunt crap. Gang work will be much better. He calls himself a 'Servant' now although he is only probationary. The big change came three months ago when he began riding with the gang. He feels safe with the gang; they understand him, accept him as he is. He has purchased a jacket and had it embroidered, but knows he cannot fly their colors yet because they have not formally inducted him.

He had driven a borrowed car to Minneapolis over the week-end, spending two days looking to find the perfect present for Brode, the 'Servants' leader. He had watched libraries, middle schools, and people leaving rock concerts until he found her. She was spectacular. The capture was easy. She helped him put his dog in the car while he was standing using two canes. Young people can be easily duped. He had delivered the Package earlier to Brode's basement. It was a struggle carrying her through the trapdoor but now it is finished and she is unhurt and secured. He had seen the bricks of money and baggies full of drugs in the basement. Soon he too would be in on the trade.

Now he is setting up a party for the gang members at a remote camp site. His nerves race in anticipation.

Even Hardin, second high in gang leadership, has promised to attend.

He is carrying a case of bourbon whiskey behind him on the bike. Other members will carry additional cases. He purchased three cases of Jack and six cases of Bud. Tonight he will establish that he deserves to lose the Probbie title and will become a full gang member. Maybe Brode will initiate him into full member status tomorrow. He is certain he will not cry out in pain, however severe the initiation rites.

CHAPTER THREE

In the quiet evening, I see a light begin to climb the rocky road to my campground. Soon it is accompanied by the irritating rumble from a road bike. A tall filthy looking man rides his bike up and parks across the fire from me.

"How you doing tonight, Buddy" I say, welcoming him.

"I ain't your buddy, Gramps." The firelight shows a bearded man with a swastika tattoo between his eyebrows. He is in a black leather jacket, WWll German style helmet complete with more swastikas, greasy looking jeans, and black boots. His body odor washes across the fire like a tsunami wave. He talks with his hands, waving them rapidly between us. A large joint hangs from his lower lip. The sweet acrid smell of marijuana floats in the air.

I wait for him to speak again. He appears to be the standard Skinhead, brutish, strong, and stupid. Small little pig eyes darting everywhere. Not good qualities to observe in a fellow camper. I have seen others like him; he is dangerous, and I fear this will not end well.

"I'm partying here tonight with a few friends," he says. "I'm expecting this to be the party of parties. Hey, you want a hit off this? No? Well, okay, where was I? Oh yeah, this party is not something you would like to attend. Now would be a real good time for you to get your crap together and get out of here." This he accentuates with his left hand circling around. "Time to be moving on, Gramps."

I put one hand down to my chair to help me stand upright.

He is standing directly across the fire from me. He unsnaps the leather lock on his knife; pulls out a six inch blade and says, "Oh, and Gramps, you might just as well leave your billfold here for me." He points the knife directly at me for emphasis. "I know you want to contribute to my party."

I take my wallet slowly from my back pocket and stoop slightly to lay it on the ground. I let it slide from my hand and when it falls to the ground, money starts spilling out. His eyes focus on the money starting to blow around. He doesn't notice my right hand closing on the fry pan handle until I straighten and fling the hot grease into his face. Both of his hands go to his face as he reels backward trying to protect his eyes from the intense heat. I pull my fillet knife. I believe that his two most vulnerable places are his throat and lower abdomen. That fat gut of his is closer to me than his throat. I deliberately aim low because I know that my thin blade will not penetrate his belt and will probably snap into two pieces if it strikes either his ribs or the chains he is wearing around his waist.

I stab deep pulling the razor sharp knife downward with a twisting slice, to cut through as much of his flesh as I can. His left hand drops rapidly to his abdomen as he tries to hold his intestines in and stem the loss of blood. He swings his blade downward rapidly with his right hand trying to cut me. His blood has already begun to run over my hand. I pull my knife hand clear and step back quickly. He goes to his knees, and then falls to his side, still trying to regain his feet while he is screaming obscenities at me. I walk behind him and assuming a baseball players stance, swing the iron fry pan against the back of his head. He is silent after the pan hits him. I hit him twice more for insurance. I can see the bones of his skull protruding from the wound. I grab his jacket with my left hand and drag him into the fire. The grease on his face explodes into flames, his jacket begins to burn. He smells even worse while he is burning but the fire should destroy any forensic evidence.

Quickly, I break down my tent, throw all my gear into the Jeep. I snatch up my wallet shoving the money into my pocket, then push his motorcycle over near the fire and tip it on top of him. I take the case of bourbon whiskey and put it into the back of the Jeep. Then I punch a hole in the bike's gas tank with a rock and drive out of the campground.

Two bikes pass me on the rocky trail going up to the campground as I am going down to the road. I hit the main road, turn right and fire off down the highway going as fast as the Jeep can roll. Within a half-mile the night blossoms into skyburst yellow and I can feel the concussive blast from the cycle's gas tank. Two hills later I turn left into a grassy lane leading to a few dark farm buildings. A little used lane with no visible lights indicates that the farm may be abandoned leaving only empty buildings. Further up the lane amid some overgrown trees, I stop the Jeep, turn off the lights and stand watching the highway.

The shakes had begun before I turned up the lane. Now they attack me violently.   My legs threaten to collapse causing me to lean on the Jeep. It is difficult to light a cigar with my hands shaking but I finally get it going and inhale a deep lungful. Death close up is a horrible thing. I smell of death. My hands reek with the rich coppery smell of his blood. The sweet greasy smell of burnt flesh clings to my clothes. That I had killed someone, actually ending his life, jars my mind and body. I have an incredible rush, feeling my life-force swelling through me.   Hands still trembling, legs still not wanting to work, I watch the two bikers thunder down the highway past my hiding place.

My first instinct is to return to the highway and take off driving west, directly away from my pursuers, but reason tells me that motorcycle gangs do not come in groups of three. In the age of cell phones, I could have an angry mob waiting for me to break cover no matter which way I try to run.

I drive forward into the farmyard and stop again. It was a good choice, the farm still appears abandoned. There is a boarded-up house, an open empty garage leaning precariously to the left, a large shed with its doors closed and padlocked. There is a drive-through grain bin; I can see the pasture gate through the open-ended grain bin. I drive through to the fence and open the gate to the pasture. I move the Jeep out onto the rough ground. While refastening the gate, I see one light moving up the farm lane. I hurry back to the Jeep and move into the pasture.

South Dakota dairy pastures are not smooth acres of lush green grass. They are waste land that the farmer has found unusable for planting. They have big rocks, deep washes, downed trees, in other words, they are Jeep trails, not heavy motorcycle trails.

Joe Stupid behind me has unlatched the gate and is roaring into the pasture after me. I can see the bike's headlights bouncing wildly behind me. I speed up to stay ahead. When I have gained twenty five yards on him, I slow the Jeep and step out. I walk back about ten yards and wait until he picks me up in his lights. When he sees me, he accelerates the bike at me. He is less than ten yards away when I fire my first round at him. I am worried that his bug shield will deflect the bullet but it punches through nicely. I suspect he is surprised when that first round hits him in the middle of the chest. It knocks him back in his saddle several inches. He leans to his right side and grabs at his boot. I quickly fire four more rounds at him. His bike turns to the left and goes over on its side five yards from me. I have used a small twenty two caliber pistol but it obviously has quite enough power to dump that clueless bastard on the ground. He is tough, though, and is still struggling even with five rounds in him. I see now that he is trying to pull a gun from his boot. His cheap helmet might have deflected my next round but I aim two inches below it, and with an additional hole in his head, he is no longer struggling. I knock out his head lamp with the butt of my pistol and take out my penlight.

This time the shakes are not as severe.

I can see blue and red flashing lights moving down the highway toward the campground long before I can hear any sirens. From where I stand it looks like three police cars and an ambulance are heading for the campsite. I want to light this guy up also to destroy any evidence, but turning him into a burning memory will draw the attention of the police. I use a small Penlight to make sure he is dead. His jacket is black leather. The back is covered with an ornate white design proclaiming him to be a 'Sabata's Servants.' There are four patches attached to the front of his jacket, one proclaims him to be 'Executioner'. This does not sound good to me. I notice that he has five tear shaped tattoos under his right eye.

Slowly, I drive forward without my lights until I crest the hill and can no longer see the campground. Then I switch on my headlights and go forward. I am still driving very slowly because I cannot risk breaking an axle or punching a hole in my gas tank. Once I reach the fence, I back off, set my parking brake, attach my forward winch to a corner fence post and pull it out. I drive through the opening provided by the ruined fence, up the side of the ditch and back onto a gravel road. I head north on a winding river road which I follow for several miles. I can tell there is a river to my right because of the long line of trees snaking along near the road.

I turn right on an entry way into a field of planted corn, circle the edge of the crops and continue through to the edge of the field next to the river. I back up into the trees on the river bank, stop the Jeep and turn the lights out. What I need now is a cigar. I get out of the Jeep, light a cigar and sit on the fender while I smoke. I know it doesn't really help me, I am still in deep shit with no clear way out, but for right now, I will enjoy my cigar. Troubles will still be here in five minutes. Sometimes, a short break and tobacco are great.

I am still trembling a little. Tonight I have come as close to being killed as any time since Vietnam. Both men were attempting to kill me. Truly for no reason other than I was in a place they wanted to be. They had believed they had the right of life and death over me simply because they were stronger and younger. If not for my previous military training and the Jeep's ability to drive over rough ground, I would probably be dead. I have evaded them tonight but I know tomorrow will be more difficult. Now I must worry about bikers and police. Both will be against me. But first things must of necessity come first. Now I must get rid of what evidence I can.

Holding my penlight in my mouth, I stick soap in my sock, wade out into the slow moving water. It's very cold and my bones hate the cold. I undress and let my clothes float way with the current leaving only my shoes and socks still on. I leave the penlight lit and toss it back to the shore. My legs are shaking with the cold. I take a deep breath, lean over as far as I am able and shove the Beretta as far into the soft bottom of the river, as I can. Being caught with that pistol would ensure a death penalty, either by jury or friends of the 'Servants' if I were locked up.

I hate to lose my pistol. It was a sweet piece of hardware seemingly made to fit my hand. It was incredibly accurate.

I soap myself down as quickly as I can to remove any traces of gunpowder. Then with stiff, unfeeling legs, I head for shore trying not to fall.   At my Jeep, I pull on my other set of clothes, a jacket, then wrap a blanket around me for warmth. I stretch out in the back and try to sleep. The dropping temperature is making it difficult to get warm. It feels like the temperature is in the low forties tonight.

I know I should surrender myself to the authorities in the morning. I have always been a law- abiding citizen–I did a tour with the Marines in Vietnam because I was patriotic. I know the right thing to do. But I certainly am not going to do it this time. The American legal system would inflict financial ruin upon me, at the least. Probably I would not live to see trial. I believe our system to be the best in the world for those who are rich, but for those who are poor or homeless, it can be a nightmare of forms, empty gestures of justice, and eventually imprisonment.   I do not have sufficient funds to bond out or hire a good attorney for long. I would be helpless, imprisoned without mobility or weapons, I would be ground to death under the gigantic wheels of the justice system and attorney greed. I am totally resolved. They will have to find and catch me – no voluntary surrender.

CHAPTER FOUR

Deputy Frank Johnson stands in the campground surrounded by yellow crime scene tape. The night before pictures had been taken of everything; the remains of the unknown biker and his bike had been removed leaving only an empty crime scene with a large scorched area. He is beginning to suspect that their first conclusion that this had been an inter-gang fight was wrong. He can see too much contradictory evidence. Somebody else has been here. The tent stake holes indicates a camper. The path is flattened down to the lake and there is fish blood, left on a rock, the bikers would not have gone down to the lake. Most of the ones he deals with avoid any contact with water.

He is using his cell phone to take pictures of the additional evidence he finds. The morning light reveals evidence hidden by the dark of night. A mind open to new possibilities can see the evidence as it actually is, not as it's twisted to fit a preconceived notion. Everything is readily visible in the morning light. His department had invested in expensive digital cameras just three years ago but technology moves ahead faster than county upgrades, and his cell phone currently gives better resolution. He also takes pictures of the tire tracks left by the four-wheeled vehicle.

"Was it really possible that one of the bikers had been killed by a civilian during a biker party?" He had no love for the gang, "Maybe someone deserves a medal," he thinks out loud.

Crows are making a racket in a nearby field. He pulls out his binoculars and watches them swarming an animal, probably a deer killed or wounded during the night. Then he sees a glint of light. The morning sun is reflecting off bright metal. "Probably nothing," he thinks, "but I'm through here anyway. I'll check it out before heading back to the paperwork."

He removes the yellow crime scene tape from the campground, and heads back to the road, turning east to the farm where he had seen the crows. He drives up the driveway to the land and buildings owned by a local farmer named Kelley. He sees the pasture gate has been left open and knows it should be closed. He gets out of his vehicle to investigate. Clearly, a car and a motorcycle had ridden into the pasture recently. He gets back into the patrol car and drives toward the crows. He sees the downed bike and the scavenged body of its rider. Getting out, he fires his pistol into the ground several times to chase the crows away.

The body lay sprawled in the morning sun. The crows had made his face unrecognizable but the deputy reads 'Executioner' on the jacket. He returns to his patrol car and called in. "Chief, I've found another body. It's in Sam Kelley's pasture near the abandoned buildings. Better bring out the evidence kit, ambulance for the body and something to transport a bike back. Also, better let Sam know that he should check his stock, apparently this gate has been open for a while. By the way, Chief, this body's jacket has 'Executioner' on it. Damn if it don't look like someone has declared war on 'The Servants'." The Deputy begins taking pictures of the crime scene. He notices the shell casings and picks them up. He rubs them together with a handkerchief then drops them back onto the ground. No sense in leaving forensic evidence that would get someone caught for this 'service to mankind.'

Then he calls his wife. "Great news, I am looking at the body of Hardin. He's been shot in the head. I don't know who did it, but thank God that bastard is finally dead. Maybe we should arrange a parade for whoever did this."

CHAPTER FIVE

Brode was impatient. Hardin, his first lieutenant and executioner, had told him earlier that a package had been delivered. It was a slow night until Ral called and said that the Probbie had been attacked and killed. Ral said he and Hardin were going after the Probbie's killer. The killer had been seen driving an older Jeep. Brode had sent several riders out to watch the main roads to the west, but he certainly was not worried. He was sure Hardin and Ral could find and take care of whoever had killed the Probbie. It was still early in the evening.

Anticipation and the delay increased the energies building up inside him. The quality, age, and sex of the package was unknown and his imagination ratcheted up his energies even higher. He continued to stay at the bar drinking with the gang and waiting for word from Hardin or Ral. In the early morning hours, he used a few lines of cocaine to steady himself.

He left the bar heading straight for the Package. At the house he moved the table, pulled the linoleum back, raised the trapdoor and went down.   She lay naked, on a pallet, bathed in harsh florescent light. Her arms were taped down to the pallets legs pushing her chest out.   Her barely protruding breasts were accentuated. Her feet were taped to a stick which forced her legs apart and the stick was tied to the table. She was gagged and blindfolded.   Brode could see her very fine pubic hair. He stroked the hair on her head. Slowly, he began to undress himself, then gently caressed her feet, gently bit each large toe. He removed the blindfold to reveal her large brown eyes, opened wide with terror. He gently licked each eye. This was looking to be the best night of his life if he could just keep himself calm enough.

Much later and totally spent, he calls the bar to say he is finished with her, then swings by the café for breakfast, devours his food rapidly, returns home, and ignoring the noise from the basement, is asleep by the time Hardin's body is found.

CHAPTER SIX

I am feeling good about being alive when that long dark night begins to lighten. I sit enjoying being warm and sleepy for a few minutes. Then I get up, shake off the sleep and turn the Jeep north heading for safer territories. If I just journey to new places like Chicago, last night will soon be only a memory. By the time the rich magenta sky has lightened to blossoming gold, I have changed my mind. Despite all the fear and anxiety I have suffered through during the night, I am feeling alive, more alive than I have since before my wife became ill. I am going back. I turn the Jeep around heading back to town. I think I will explore just a little.

Midwest towns spread out. The population of Tanley could probably fit into one square block of New York City, but here in the wide open west everything can use more room. Tanley is bordered on the south by highway 60. It's surrounded on the other three sides by section roads. It is still totally within the section but continues to reach out generationally. The stores stretch four blocks along Main

Street.   They all have descriptive signs telling of their business, garage, food, etc.   The signs remain although many of the businesses are now defunct.   Hard times have come even to the small towns. They mostly consist of small buildings fronted by larger facades. From its start on the highway, Main Street is eleven blocks long. It's anchored to the north by the grain elevator.

The elevator covers a full square block, rising into the morning sky like an Aztec Sun Altar. It is the economic center of the community, serviced daily by the farmers who devote their lives and crops to feed it.

The Townies spend their lives servicing the farmers. They build their two story wood frame houses and spend their lives on their own plot of land. A garage behind each house, a sidewalk in front, bordered by short white picket fences. Every lot seems to have at least two trees and is covered with well-tended grass.

One house stands out for its lack of paint, absence of garage, a tilting awning extends from one side, unkempt yard, muddy driveway. It has no sidewalks.   I think this must be the Witches' house on Halloween.   It is on the northwestern corner of the town.

I park in front of the small clapboard cafe on the southern edge of town. It sits on a gravel parking lot. The Breakfast Nook has been around for a long time. It, like the town, has a worn appearance. It smells of old grease and ammonia cleaners. The front entrance has a screen door for summer only use and wooden door which rings a bell when opened. It makes a muffled bang each time it is released. A red Formica counter sits in front of ten stools. They are accompanied across a narrow aisle by four tired looking booths. The benches are covered with hard red and white plastic. The standard black and white checkered tile covers the floor. The walls are covered with signs advertising soft drinks, food, and food prices. I slide easily into a booth, order coffee and 'The Breakfast Mess,' a local concoction described as stacked hash browns covered with two eggs, and cheese all smothered with sausage gravy and accompanied by two pieces of toast. It smells great cooking and tastes better when the waitress, an older lady with thinning gray hair and suspicious eyes, finally serves it. The coffee is perfection.

There had been a biker, wearing a black leather jacket with an ornate design on the back

saying, 'Sabata's Servants', sitting at the counter eating breakfast when I first came in. I doubt that he noticed me. He gave the appearance of a very tired man. He dropped a ten on the counter and left before my coffee arrived. I did not talk to him. The bikers in this town do not appear to be friendly.

Other people begin filtering in. I am listening trying to pick up any news on the killings but nothing is being said. The people talk about the weather, orders, health, etc., nothing of any interest. Paying too much attention to everything else, I am surprised when I look up and a deputy sheriff is standing by my booth. My heart immediately begins racing. I may have a heart attack right here. 'Just stay calm,' I think, 'Just stay calm.'

"Mind if I sit?" He asks as he slides in across from me.

"Please," I respond. Not much else to say since he is already sitting there. "Good morning, Officer."

"Just get into town?" He asks.

"I was just driving through on my way west and got hungry. This looked like a good place to eat."

He looks at me for a minute, then glances around and speaks softly. "My name is Frank Johnson. I'm a deputy with this county. I came to find you before you get yourself killed. You should know that if I can find you this easy, so can the 'Servants'. I am not here to arrest you, I'm here to keep you alive, if I can. You are putting yourself and the customers in here in a great deal of danger just sitting here."

"Why would you think that?" I ask.

He again just looks at me. Then patiently he explains, "All of the people who have walked in this morning, except you, can see you are from out of town with those Florida tags. Also, every farmer here knows that you have driven that Jeep through a pasture recently by looking at the weeds and the mud stuck to it. You do not pick up much plant life or real estate driving on the highway. I know you killed those two bikers last night. I know you drove through that pasture and busted that fence. You camped by the bank of the Jim river. Now I suggest you quit playing the innocent fool, pay for your food, and follow me out of here. We need to get you off the streets before the wrong eyeballs see you."

I had changed from feeling pretty good to completely stupid in five minutes.

"You really should trust me, I'm the one good chance you have to get out of this alive. Now are you with me or are you going to sit here waiting for the 'Servants'?'

Sometimes you have to trust your instincts. "I am with you."

"Then let's go." He throws ten dollars on the table top and walks out to his car.

I get into the Jeep and follow him four blocks into town, then pull into the open empty garage he is parked next to.

He walks around my Jeep pulling several corn leaves, a fragment of a corn stalk, and some weeds off the Jeep.

"You will need to get this baby washed but it looks better," he says.

His house is an older two-story wooden building. Its paint is faded and peeling, still somewhat white, with a newer attached two-stall garage. There is a light blue sedan sitting in the other stall. It looks to be in good shape but the style is at least ten years old. He walks into the garage, runs the door down behind him. I follow him as he walks into his kitchen.

A pretty blond lady, wearing no makeup, is sitting at the table in what looks like a nightgown covered over by a terrycloth robe. She has a cup of coffee sitting in front of her. Smiling at us, she pours out two additional cups of coffee. She has a warm pretty smile. I feel like I already know her. The kitchen has dark wood cabinets wrapped around the side opposite the table. A small window is cut into the middle of the cabinets. It looks down on a white porcelain sink. A stove is sitting against the wall in the left corner. Six chairs, covered in gray plastic are around a gray plastic table with a three inch chrome lip. I wonder if they have kids now, or are planning for kids in the future.

"Coffee, guys, " she asks?

"Please, for both of us," Frank responds. "This is my wife, Jennie. We have been hooked for a little over nine years now.

I say, "My name is Matt. I have been traveling for a while."

"Matt," he stops me, "I know you are worried and not sure you can trust us yet but you haven't got a many options to choose from. You need help to get through this. Your Jeep is covered in Jim River mud, your winch is still loose from when you used it to break that fence down. You still have parts of corn stalks hanging on your rear bumper. Even a casual observer knows you drove through a corn field this morning, and I am a trained professional investigator. You should understand, by now, that I know what you did last night. Jenny and I are your friends. I am not going to arrest you. You have to start trusting me, though. You will have many more friends in town when they find out what you did, but the 'Servants' have their friends too. We have a lot to talk about and little time to make our preparations."

"Thanks for the coffee, Jennie. It's great, but I could use something a little stronger in it. If you have it" I say.

"Sorry, I have no booze in the house right now," says Frank.

"Wait just a second." I go out to the Jeep and pull two bottles of Jack Daniels from the case, bring them in and put them on the table. Slowly, I twist the cap off the top of one bottle and pour about an inch into my coffee.

"It's been a hard night," I say. "You two have a lovely house. Thanks for taking me in. First of all, Frank, I do trust you. If I didn't trust you, I wouldn't have come. It's just that I am still very confused and uncertain as to why you would want to help a stranger. You see, it's very strange, I have never seen myself as a killer. But, at the same time, I feel great that I killed those two and am still alive. Somehow though, I also feel horrible that I killed them. Now you two, very nice people have invited a killer into your home."

When I was in college, I worked nights cleaning at a hog slaughter plant. We were very efficient in the use of the hog. Almost everything was used. They claimed they used everything but the squeal and the shit. The squeal went off into the ether. The shit was flushed out of the hog's intestines and it was collected in a six foot by six foot holding tank about two feet deep. I shoveled that tank out every night. Killing those two was like I was cleaning the human equivalent of that tank. So I say, from me to you, fuck those Neo Nazi bastards."

"I know what you mean," says Frank. "I can tell you that those two weren't worth keeping alive. You really were flushing a toilet. They deserved what they got. The world is better without them. What worries me is that if anyone in the gang or any of their friends gets a good description of you or your Jeep, they will be after you until you are dead. 'Servants' are affiliated with outlaw gangs across the nation, so there is nowhere you can go and be safe," he is watching me while he sips his coffee.

Jennie turns to look directly at me. She has tears in her eyes and her voice cracks when she speaks. "Thank you for killing him, for killing Hardin. You may feel a little bad about it but I certainly don't. I feel free without that rock around my neck. I will always be grateful to you."

Frank explains, "That second guy you took out last night, his name was Hardin. He was the executioner for the gang. He did their killing for them. He was an animal, a bona fide beast. Two years ago he ran over our seven year old son, Jack. as he was walking to school. That bastard stopped his bike, picked Jack up, threw him to the side of the road, then rode on, like our Jack was of no value. Jennie and I have hated him and the gang since. The City has brought him to trial two times but has failed to convict him. Hung juries both times. Too much pressure brought against the jury members' families." Frank continues, "We were seriously considering a move. I would quit my job, sell the house and find someplace to live that has a lot more sunshine in it. Otherwise, we were going to kill that mongrel ourselves regardless of the consequences. You saved us from that; now let us help save you. And I don't mean by praying over you."

I had finished my coffee and filled the cup half up with whiskey. "Think I will skip the coffee this time."

"Here's the thing, I wasn't being a hero or an avenger when this all happened. That first guy was trying to rob me. The second guy was trying to run me down. I just did what I had to do to save my own skin."

"That first biker sure made a mistake taking you for an easy mark," says Frank. "But I've always believed that the members of that gang have a collective brain the size of a walnut."

"Thank you again," said Jenny, "I don't care why you killed them. Thank you."

Frank said, "I picked up your casings at the scene and wiped them clean. They can never be traced to you. I will let you know if any of the bullets themselves are salvageable for forensic evidence and can be traced to your pistol, but it's going to take some time for that, at least a few days."

"I threw the pistol. No worry there; it will never be found," I said. "What really worries me is that I do not like to drag you both into this. Perhaps it would be better if I drove out now, heading north on back roads. I think I would be safe enough."

"You wouldn't travel too far before they found you. Too many eyes. They have a lot of friends you wouldn't suspect."

"How many gang members are there?"

Frank said, "I know there are at least twenty of them. They control the drugs in this area. Plus, I think they have a few places where they cook meth."

"I don't understand how they could have many friends."

"They have been here for about five years. They built up a pretty good drug trade. Now they have branched off into the sex trade also. They lawyer up in a heartbeat. They use intimidation to further their needs. They have threatened and roughed up more than one witness. Money and fear are two powerful motivators. They have family members, relatives, and girlfriends who help watch for them. I suspect they have an informer in the courthouse, also."

The phone rang. Jennie jumped, answered it, then handed it to Frank. "It's the office." Frank mumbled into the receiver, hung up, "I've got to get in to work. Sheriff is going ballistic. Your visit has really stirred up the office."

"The best thing to do now, Matt, is stay with us until this all cools down. Maybe, if we are lucky we can get you through the next week in one piece. But you gotta plan on being here at least a week or two, then we'll send you out early one morning. We can say Jennie's uncle is visiting from Florida. No one should be too suspicious of that. Jack's room is already made up. Get some sleep now. We can talk more when I get off work, but now I got to get back before Thatcher really goes ballistic."

He shows me to a side room filled with young boy's stuff; basketball hoop, a football, pictures, trophies, and a single bed. Perfect. I stand for a while under the shower, then I go out to the Jeep to get my medications and am asleep within ten minutes of Frank's leaving. Every time someone says meds, anymore, the assumption is psychopath, but my meds are for cholesterol, restless leg syndrome, and a small chemo dose from prostate surgery last year. Actual medical meds. Seems like my doctor is trying to keep me alive not just sane. Despite his advice, I do like an occasional cigar. I know they are bad for me because I can feel my heart racing but damned if I'm not going to die anyway. I like smoking a cigar.

The evening is starting to darken by the time I wake up. For several minutes I do nothing. I lie there stretching, relaxing, thinking. Just enjoying the security and comfort of being in a house. The noises and smells provide a sense of safety. Then I dress and walk into the kitchen.

Jenny is at the stove cooking something. I am instantly ravenous. "It smells heavenly."

"Frank will be back soon," Jenny says. "Want something to take the edge off?" She slides a sandwich over to me. I wonder at the compassion and love shown a virtual stranger by this wonderful woman.

"Thanks, I'm famished."

"It feels good having you here, cooking and caring for someone again. The strain of this last two years has been tough. Don't mean to worry you about it, but I need to talk to someone and you are here. Got to pay for that sandwich somehow," she smiles that radiant smile. "You look like you can keep a confidence. "

"Jennie, I don't know anyone else in town. I can't spread a rumor even if I wanted to."

"There is that," she says. "It's been a tough fight for Frank and me, day in and day out. We

have been like two hostile camps in the same house. The anger and depression just kept eating at us. We almost split up several times. But I think we are going to make it now. I noticed a huge change in my guy when he came home for lunch. His face, his posture, he is just more like the real Frank. Actually kissed me when he walked in. He kissed me. It's been a long time since that's happened. By the way, he said there had been a lot of road action by the 'Servants.'

Glad you stayed. We have to keep our hero safe."

Later that night after dinner, Frank and I go for a walk. I am restless. I need fresh air, a little exercise and a cigar.

In the cool dark of the evening, my breath is just visible if I exhale towards a street lamp. Perfect night to just stroll and talk. I hold the railing to maintain my balance and step down slowly to the sidewalk. My left knee still stiff after surgery does not bend like it should. Frank's lawn is nicely manicured with a border of what looks like blueberry bushes on the inside of his fence. When I reach the sidewalk, I stop to light my cigar. I still use matches when possible, it seems to make the whole process more enjoyable. Matches blow out easier and therefore require more attention to get the cigar properly lit. Frank and Jennie live in a nice area, the street is clean, the houses well-kept and there is a nice tossing of trees to provide beauty and shade. We walk slowly enjoying the evening and the company.

"Sure glad you saw my car at the Nook. It's been great meeting you two. With the hot showers, great food, and a real bed, this has been a stay in paradise."

"No prob. Glad we can help."

"Tell me a little more about the gang, Frank. Do they have a central meeting place, like a house or a bar?"

"They hang at a shit hole called Chicks. I told you about the drugs; they also have two cheesy strip bars and a quick trip motel with each bar. They control the girls. We should have cleaned them out of the county years ago. But they have big bucks. We are told to keep hands off unless we see a drug sale in progress."

"Damn, that seems strange here in the bible belt."

"We were told they bring a lot of money into the state from the hunters. And I have to admit this area is swarming with horny drunk men during pheasant hunting season. There are not that many birds here in the southern part of the state."

"Just seems all wrong to me," I say.

"There has to be a pay-off higher up. I believe that Sheriff Thatcher is honest, but I don't trust everyone above him. They can't all be crooked but some are. If someone wasn't helping them they wouldn't get such low bail and practically avoid prosecution altogether."

"Is their bar located near here?"

"Everything is close in this small town. We'll walk that way and I can show you."

The bar sits on a large macadam paved lot. A large dumpster is located at the rear left of the lot. Several hard scrabble trees are growing on each of the front corners. The door at the front of the bar is the largest. There are doors on the left side and rear of the building also. The one in back leads past the restroom and the left side door exits from the room the pool tables are in, at least that's how I see it in my mind. Ten to twelve motorcycles are parked around the lot. A large window covered with ads and neon signs takes up much of the front of the bar. Over the door is a small sign designating this as CHICKS BAR. This bar is not designed to attract customers from off the street, nor do I think they attract many chicks.

"You said it right, Frank. It looks like a shit hole." I finish my cigar. We slowly head back to the house. "If you don't mind Frank, I will stay for another week at least. Then if everything stays quiet I will head out for northern Minnesota, maybe cross into Canada. I've always wanted to drive across Canada."

"We don't mind your staying at all."

Seemed like good plans at the time. Plans can change.

There is tension thick in the morning air when I get up. They become quiet as I enter the kitchen. Jennie turns and looks at the stove, while Frank keeps his eyes averted.

"What is it?" I ask. "Come on, no secrets before morning coffee."

Frank finally answers, "At first light this morning, our office received a call about a body found ten miles east of here, over by Lester. It was an older man who had been run off the road, beaten severely, his arms were obviously broken. He was tied to a barb-wire fence with an additional loop strung around his neck. As he tried to escape, the loop kept tightening until he strangled himself with the wire. The sheriff thinks he may have been targeted because he was driving a Jeep."

I feel my heart stop. My brain is imploding. Suddenly my whole world has changed. My beliefs, my values, all is askew. Where is Right? Where is Justice? I am alone watching my life turn completely. Have I become am Death, or has Death attached itself to me. One unfortunate man has died because he drove the same type of car as me. My actions and reactions have caused his death. Clearly I see the road behind as a trail of death stretching mist like into dust. The path of my future appears clearly; blackness is coming. Those I know, those I touch, those affected by my aura are doomed. I have to leave this place. The house is shrinking around me. I fight for breath. Finally, I stand and go outside. Light a cigar. Look at the morning sun. Tanley has been hit by violence without reason. A man has suffered badly and then was killed. I hear him crying for revenge. I must act on this. The 'Servants' think they have stopped me when they killed that innocent. It's time they discover there are consequence for such actions.

I tell Frank and Jennie I must leave. I will call soon but for now I must be alone. I start to pack up all my gear. "And Frank, tell your Undertaker to stock up on coffins, he is going to need them."

CHAPTER SEVEN

I am in my Jeep and on the road in less than five minutes. I drive north on state and county roads until I came to Tripp Lake. I sit for a few minutes watching the water, planning. It's easier to plan while watching water. I head out to the main highway and continue north another fifteen miles to Parkston. I stop at the Credit Union there and withdraw five thousand dollars. Perhaps too much but I am unsure when I can get back or that I will need money at all after the next two weeks. I have to wait a short time while they contact my bank but I am in no hurry now. Now with money, I fill my Jeeps gas tank and run it through the car wash attached to the station. I visit the Catholic Church while I am there. I sit in the back pew and pray for several minutes. While I am not overly religious, I have visited this Church several times with my wife over the years. It is associated with the Grotto of the Redemption. It is certainly one of the most beautiful Churches in the world. As I leave, I stuff $500 into the poor box near the door. I'm unsure why.

I know I need firepower. I want a handgun but know I can't buy one out of the state of my residence, long barreled guns can be purchased out of state because they are used for hunting. A shotgun is the obvious choice for personal protection. I want two shotguns, tactical preferably. Not too sure if I want to get both at one time as I do not want to raise suspicions. A clerk will be less likely to remember me if I buy only one. I drive around town looking for stores. I pick out a large chain store with several people at the counter. One clerk comes over and offers to help me. I say, "I am looking for a home defense kind of shotgun."

"We have a good selection, Remington is good, Mossberg is good also, but our best is the Benelli M4. Its reliability is legendary. For the last ten years, it's been standard Marine Corps issue because of its reliability. They use it in the mud, cold, and rain, and it never jams. So, you can rest assured that it won't jam in your home, either. Easily an excellent choice. Traditionally sells for about two thousand but I have a used one on sale right now for sixteen fifty. It's in beautiful shape. Want to see it?'"

I look at a Mossberg, a Remington, and the Benelli. I take my time, spending most of it looking at the Remington. There are a lot of gun buyers here and I can see buying two guns will not raise suspicions. When the clerk returns, I tell him I want a sling strap for both, and a cartridge band for the stock to carry extra shells. I tell him I will take the Remington and the Benelli with everything, and I will give him two thousand for the lot if he throws in a couple of boxes of twelve gauge bird shot.

Now he begins to hem and haw. "I need at least twenty two fifty for all. This isn't a non-profit business."

I say, "Here's the thing. I can go with just the Remington, that's all I need. But I do like the Benelli." We both know he will make the most money on the used Benelli. He doesn't take long to fold. He get two thousand; I get everything I wanted. We both feel like we got a deal. It takes a half an hour to complete the paper work and since they are both long barreled guns, I can take them with me.

While I am walking around, I find two skinning knives with three inch blades and a used Marine K-BAR. I offer him fifty for all three and he jumps at it. Now, I am feeling better. I drive to down town Mitchell and search out a pawn shop. The clerk/owner watches me from behind his cage. This guy has some good stuff. I buy three boxes of buckshot gauge shotgun shells, two boxes of shotgun slugs, two used knives which he had listed for a good price, and a pair of tactical ceramic knuckle gloves. I see he has a Mosin-Nagant rifle for sale. They only want one hundred and fifty dollars and that includes 20 rounds of ammo. The Nagant is a Russian-made WWll sniper rifle that is remarkably accurate for the price. I talk to the owner and show him what I want. I offer two hundred and fifty for the lot. He pulls out the form and starts completing it. Since it is a long gun also, I am able to buy it and carry it right away. I ask the man where the local Goodwill is located.

I find it easily. I need new clothes. I am wearing the only clothes I own. I buy two long sleeved shirts, two tee shirts and two pair of used jeans. While I am there, I also find some socks, a couple of used caps, an old baseball bat, used binoculars, and a light jacket I get out of there with all that loot for only ninety six dollars. What a buy.

Behind the Goodwill store, I toss the boxes for the shotguns in the dumpster. I put on my gloves and then load them with buckshot and place them into the back of the Jeep. The boxes for the knives also go into the dumpster; I load the Nagant with an eight round clip. I am feeling safer. I cover everything in back with the clothes I had purchased.

CHAPTER EIGHT

By this time, Brode is ass deep in gang shit. The two dead members combined with the killing of the old guy who could have been the perpetrator throws fire into the gang's collective. Losing his Executioner is tough on him personally as Hardin was a true friend and trusted second-in-command. Now he needs a new Executioner, not an easy position to fill. Brode's most reliable member currently is named Joe. His appearance is deceiving. He has long hair, tied behind his back, a thick brow with long broad nose accentuated his sparse mustache.

He wears casual clothes and has a quiet demeanor. His short stature belies his awesome strength. He has thick muscular legs and a broad chest. By the time he had gotten out of reform school, at age sixteen, he could answer for himself as a mechanic. By age eighteen, he had bought his first motorcycle and began riding with the 'Servants'.

Brode became impressed by Joe when he had to handle three collegiate football players who were getting too hands-on with the girls. Joe told them to sit, quiet down, and keep their hands off the girls. They had laughed and tried to crowd him. He hit each of them one time, then dragged their inert bodies out to the parking lot. Brode could hear bones break with each of the blows. He acquired his gang name, 'Blood,' after a long dry run, when he cracked the top off a long neck bottle on a rock and drank the whole beer ignoring the blood pouring out of the cuts on his lips. The gang called him, 'Blood,' since that day. It's a name he likes. Blood is one of his most ardent skinheads, even if he does have long hair.

Now Brode calls Blood to the front of the bar. Pours a glass of Jack for himself, Blood, and all the gang members present. "I propose we promote Blood to Executioner. Anyone want to challenge him, now is the time." No one wants to challenge him, Brode holds his glass high and says. "You were and are our brother, now you are our 'Executioner,' also. "

At least something is moving forward.

The headman was putting pressure on Brode to reduce the visibility of the gang's violence. The two biker deaths' were very bad for their image and must be avenged. But the death of the older man was putting too much fear into the community. Business was staying away. The bars and the girls were so slow, some nights it was not worth opening them. When he had checked on them one evening, the girls were playing cards. He had never seen it that quiet before. The agitation in the community was cutting into the drug sales, also. Narcotics sold better when the cops were sitting in the station, not driving up and down the roads.

The gang itself is restless. Violence sparks more violence. The killing has not satisfied their blood lust. Brode is stepping carefully; there are egg shells surrounding him, and he does not like to step carefully. A mission for his men will help. "Let's make sure we get this gray-haired piece of shit." He sent three members east, three west, and three north, to search, to make sure they had caught and killed the right old man. "Look for campers. That old fuck could be sitting in a tent laughing at us now. But check out old men in Jeeps, too, never trust, never trust. If they ain't in the gang, never trust."

Personally, he didn't believe they had done the right guy. They had gone out filled with blood lust. They killed the first poor bastard who even looked close. But once everyone believed that the old shithead was dead, everything would return to business as usual. There are a lot of them old turds around and thinning out the herd wouldn't hurt. He usually wouldn't care if they got the right guy or not but this time it was personal. The bastard that killed Hardin had to die, and suffer a shitload before he died.

Once the bikers rode, he has a few beers with the remaining members, then he goes to the house. It is well after midnight and no one has reported any action. The Package is still alive. She has to be tough to make it through that long night. She has suffered plenty. Clearly she has more strength than Brode gave her credit for. The gang members used her badly. She is bruised. Her face is swollen. She has an anal tear and seven of the gang members have taken fingers as souvenirs. One has taken an ear. She still moaning lowly. He cuts her loose, then carries her over to the freezer and stuffs her inside. She barely fit on top of the others already there. She has been so beautiful, Brode knows he will remember her.

CHAPTER NINE

I drive down to the shores of Lake Tripp. Lake Tripp is a smallish lake. Three miles long and about half a mile wide. The county has set up a series of small campgrounds around the edges of the lake. The first one, I look at has an entry road about three blocks long leading to fifteen camp sites. It is all well forested with cottonwood and cedar trees. The second site I drive into is immediately south of the first one. It is smaller with an entry road of only one block and has five sites. This site is two hundred yards from the other site. These two campgrounds are set up to be accessible but not too close together. Campers from one site are separated by the distance, but can easily walk up and visit with the other site. Both campgrounds are deserted and neither has been maintained for at least three weeks. The grass is long, several tree branches have broken and are laying on the ground or still hanging from the trees. Leaves are thick on the ground.

I decide to use the first campground on the southernmost site. I clean my site up as best I can, break a lot of the fallen wood into smaller pieces, and have a happy little fire going before long. I set up my tent, back the Jeep as far as possible into the trees where it cannot be easily seen. I check the loads in my weapons. It's always better to double check. Taking one shotgun and my fly rod, I walk to the shore. I soon have a fine Northern Pike landed. This Royal Coachman fly is just a great fly for freshwater fish. A little butter, a little salt and this fish is delicious. Especially with a glass of lake water. I add a couple of shots of Biker Whiskey to purify it.

When twilight sets in, I leave the fire burning, take my blanket out of the tent and crawl back into the long grass about fifteen yards from my camp site. I wrap myself with the blanket, holding the Benelli loaded and cocked near my side, take my medications, and fall into a deep sleep.

I awake to the rumble of a big road bike. I can see a headlight turn into the campground, shining onto my tent. The bike stops and the lights go out. Now my night is lit by a half-moon providing only blacks and grays. I slip on my glasses tying to make clear what I am looking at. Night vision is not my strength but I can make out where the shape of a bike is parked in the night. There is someone moving around near my tent. I extend my Benelli toward the tent. I have it loaded with buckshot.

A flashlight clicks on; it's pointed at my tent. "Come on out of that tent, Rabbit." He pulls my tent down by the stake ropes and throws it to one side. "Where are you hiding, little Rabbit?" He walks down towards the outhouse searching for me. I hear him crunching through the dried grass and leaves near the shore line. He shines the flashlight around and I turn my head shutting my eyes. I am afraid that if he shines the light in my eyes or on my glasses the light will be reflected back to him. I try to remain as motionless as I possible. When the light moves, I look back at him. He is methodical and steady, walking slowly, kicking logs, watching the grass. He is circling to my left and comes within three yards of me. Then he puts the light right on me. "There you are little Rabbit."

Since the Benelli is already aimed at his legs, I pull the trigger. He flies backwards as if hit by a car. I stand slowly, adjusting to the dark, regaining my balance. I pick up his flashlight to see how he is. His right leg is hanging on by skin only; his left leg is bloody but still fully attached. He lies semi-conscious, moaning. I take a pistol from his hand. I go to the Jeep, throw the pistol in the back, grab my duct tape and return to him. I wrap his wrists together with the duct tape from the top of his thumbs up to his elbows. I put an additional three strong loops around his wrists. Then I tape up his right leg above the thigh. I use a stout stick and tape one end to his thigh. I twist the stick until his stump quits bleeding, then tape the ends of the stick down to his thigh, also. I do not want him bleeding to death before I can talk to him. I cut off his left pants leg. I tape up the holes in his left leg to prevent more blood loss.

Foolishly, I am careless. I put my arm too close to his hands. He grips my left wrist with his left hand, wounded and tightly taped, he is still incredibly strong. His grip is viselike. It feels like he is close to breaking the bones in my wrist. I pull my knife out with my right hand and whack his fingers. The pressure on my arm releases immediately as his fingers are almost severed. I just let his fingers bleed.

"How are you doing tonight, Rabbit-hunter?" I ask him.

I grab his left leg and start dragging him to the campfire but he tries wildly to kick me. Threshing and bucking, he is coming too close. So I drop his leg and pick up the tape again. I run three loops of duct tape around my hand and up to my elbow. I take it off my arm and squeeze it together. Now I have an sixteen inch loop of tape which I place around his neck. I drag him by the head over to the fire ring. He is busy choking and gasping. I put wood on the smoldering fire to get enough light to see better.

He watches with eyes glistening hate. He is not talking yet.

"You having fun yet Rabbit-hunter? You going to talk to me? My first question is easy. Did you come out by yourself or are others with you?"

He glares silently.

"Damn, son," I say, "hope you didn't hurt your mouth when you fell back there." I pull out my knife. "Let's get a look in that mouth of yours."

He refuses to open it right away so I rap him sharply across the teeth with the handle of the knife. I don't need to rap him the second time. His lips bleeding and several fractured teeth help him to reconsider his silence.

"I came alone."

I don't believe him. Still, I can't hear any bikes so I feel pretty safe yet.

"Hey, hey, hey. Glad to see you can talk because I have some questions for you. If you tell me what I want to know and answer with the truth, I might even let your sorry ass live."

Ten minutes later, I pull him over to a scrub tree. I cut his right leg all the way off. Then I tape it between his hands. I stand him up and tape his neck to a young cottonwood tree.

He is now standing on his left leg holding his right leg in his hands.

"If your left leg is strong enough to stand until help comes, you should be okay. If you do survive, tell your leader that I am coming for him. I will not be this nice to him."

I use his flashlight, pick up all of the gear I can find scattered around and put everything into my Jeep. Then I reload my Benelli with slugs. The other shotgun still has buck shot. I push his bike over near the fire, punch a small hole in the gas tank with my knife. I get into the Jeep and I drive south to the next campground.

The night lights up with an exploding bike. It is an encouraging sight. If his friends are within ten miles, they should hear the blast or see the light.

I drive to the site within the southern camp that is closest to the burning bike. Then back up all the way to the shore.

I grab the Remington, load it with slugs and slowly walk north on the shore sand and out into the shallow water towards the fire. I walk slowly and very carefully as a fall now could end up being fatal. I cannot trip over the grass and get a broken limb in the dark. When I reach the prior campsite, I put the shotgun down and pick up a handful of mud to cover my face and hands. With my gun at the ready, safety off, I stand in the shadows behind the outhouse waiting.

Within ten minutes, two bike lights are shining down the entrance to the campground. I hear the bikes stop, see the headlights switch off. There is still a low level of light provided by the fire. I move slowly out until I can see the two gang members going over to Rabbit-hunter. One biker is trying to unfasten the injured man's neck from the tree. The other biker has knelt down and is doing something to his leg.

I call out, "Stop where you are and raise your hands."

Both men stop and look at me. Clearly they can see the shotgun which I have pointed midpoint between the two.

"Raise your hands and drop to your knees. I am taking you into Mitchell to the State Police."

Neither one drops or raises his hands. They turn and look at each other. Not a good sign that things will go my way.

They attempt to move apart, one to the left, one to the right hoping that I will be confused and miss my shot. At the first movement, I shoot the biker to the left in the middle of his chest. Pull over to the other biker who has glanced my way before turning to run. I shoot at him, and he spins further to his left but is still running. I am sure I hit him. I see his pistol flare as he fires at me. I aim at the flash and fire again. He slams hard into the ground and lays still. Both men lay totally motionless. Everything is suddenly very still and quiet. Quite unnerving after the rapidity of the action and roar of the shotgun.   I walk up to them. Turn on the flashlight.

The first guy has been hit by a slug with only a half inch radius when it entered his chest, but it began expanding immediately.   It pushed his sternum further into his chest catching his heart and aorta.   All three keep traveling through him. They push hard on his spine and blow out a portion of his spine about the size of a saucer.

The first slug hit the second guy in his right shoulder, it went straight through and broke the bone in his upper arm spinning him away from me. The second slug caught him in the throat and tore out a few of the vertebra in his neck, then exited his body through a hole about as big as a silver dollar. Definitely a fast way to die.   There is no chance either is alive. I pull them over to the fire, one at a time. A quick search shows they both have pistols. The first guy I shot had eighty dollars on him and the second had almost two hundred dollars. I put their money in my pocket. They won't need it. Then I push their motorcycles on top of them. I step back about ten yards and put a slug through both gas tanks. By the time I walk back the two hundred yards to my Jeep there is another very loud explosion.

Count now is four dead.   One disabled permanently. Time for a cigar. I know he missed but I can still see the gun aiming and firing at me when I close my eyes. Only luck still has me here breathing. I really dislike people shooting at me.

I drive into Tripp to call Frank. "I know it's late but I can be there in twenty five minutes, if that's okay with you."

"I will leave the garage door open."

He is still up sitting at the table when I come in. He waits until the garage door is closed.

"Run into a little trouble?"

"There are three less members of the 'Servants'.   Two dead for sure. The third is out of action. I am starting to worry about how big this rat's nest is going to be and how far we will have to go to eliminate it. Want to talk?"

"Sure, what's up?'

"The last two guys I shot. They were just going to help their friend. I tried to arrest them and take them into the State Troopers. But they turned on me so I shot them, killed them. Maybe I should have tried to wound them. But then, I thought of the old man they murdered because they wanted to kill me. So I just wasted them. Probably, I would be convicted of murder if brought to court. But at the same time, there is no doubt in my mind they were out looking to kill me. I am certain that I did the right thing. I just as certain as I was when the older man in the Jeep was killed. I know I am on the right path, the side of good. I believe in spite of everything that we have every right to attack and kill those who are attacking and trying to kill us. I do not want to kill anyone who is innocent, but I gotta say those members I have killed so far are not innocent. Any of them would have killed me in a heartbeat. I killed my enemies in Vietnam, but only as combatants, I always felt if I met them at a bar somewhere, we would have talked and had a beer together. Not so with these animals. I wouldn't drink with them. I know you as a police officer have different rules and I don't want to force you into anything you are totally against."

"If they had 'Sabata's Servant' on their jacket, they were sent out to find and kill you. But I am glad you understand my dilemma. I should be having problems here. I am sworn to protect people, not just good people, all people. Everything I knew before you came tells me you should stop. Violence begets violence. You have changed that in me. I know the end results of this course are not predictable, anything can happen. I am terrified that this could turn around and get Jennie killed, also. That would kill me too. But the fact is, life has no guarantees. I am with you all the way."

"The Sheriff wants to get me, doesn't he?"

"For either of the first two deaths. He doesn't know about the others yet. And any one of four deaths would mean life behind bars."

"I feel now that I should just leave, or I should deal with Brode and then leave. I decided on the way here that I would leave that decision to you."

"Oh, thanks a lot." For the first time since I met him, Frank smiles. "Leave all the easy stuff to me. Matt, let's you and me destroy this gang. I know what my oath said, but I have to be on the side of good. I am with you."

"Okay with me, nice to know I have someone I can count on." I say. "Want to see what I got tonight?" I pull out the three pistols and lay them on the table. "I'm beginning to feel like an arsenal. Hope you have some ammo around."

He picks up the first gun. It is a forty caliber Glock with a seventeen round clip. "This is what I carry on the job, very good durable weapon." He goes to a cupboard drawer and brings a box of ammunition back to the table. He fills the clip, slaps the clip in and racks a round into the chamber.

Then he picks up a Sig Sauer nine millimeter with a ten round clip. "Fuck, this guy put some money into his weapon. This is a beauty." He gets a box of nine millimeter rounds and tops off the rounds in the clip, then racks a round into the chamber. "This thing has a great feel."

"You can have it if you want it. You know I have no use for it."

"No thanks. Without knowing the history, I could get caught carrying a murder weapon. It would be difficult to explain," he says.

"Frank, get serious. When was the last time anyone checked your weapon?"

"You think maybe I am being too careful?"

"You're so anal it's lucky you can squeeze a fart out of that tight ass."

"You probably right, but I'll still pass ont the Sig."

The last pistol is a six shooter, a three-fifty-seven Ruger revolver. "I don't have ammo for this one but I can get it tomorrow. Be careful though, this will have a hell of a kick. Of course, the good part is it can probably drop an elephant."

"I want the Ruger." I say. "Mind if I sleep here tonight?"

"Nope, you know the way. I will see you in the morning."

I get my meds, shower for at least ten minutes, very hot, and slip into bed. I start to plan ahead but drop off in seconds.

CHAPTER TEN

I wake early, dress quietly, and leave the house through the rear door. The sky is beginning to lighten in the east. A ruby haze lies over the streets. It's cool out this morning, and I can see my breath when I exhale. I know any stranger walking alone in a small town is a focal point of attention for those who live here. So, I walk slowly being just another old guy out for a morning stroll. My clothing is worn jeans, tee shirt, the mandatory seed corn cap, and old well-used running shoes, all designed to blend in. I walk slowly watching the town unfold before me. My back is stiff and painful. I feel awkward, bending forward a little at the waist. I shuffle more than stride for several blocks. Gradually, the dried wang leather of my back warms up and begins to ease. The pain finally leaves.

I see lights beginning to flicker on in the houses I pass. Small town life begins anew. The elevator doors stand open already. Farmers wake long before dawn to beginning their sacred rigid ritual of chores. Then their trucks are moving. Corn is being delivered from the fields to the elevator. Corn is being delivered from the elevator to the trains. Trains deliver it to the nation. Corn is the very life blood of the small mid-western town, and at times seems like the life blood of the American food chain.

I continue westward. The last house has a motorcycle under its overhang. I believe this house is the answer. This is my epiphany from last night. The house is so different from all the other houses in town that it must belong to the leader of the gang itself. It's such a dump that I would have thought an older welfare couple lived here except for the huge Harley Davidson under the overhang. It is an awe-inspiring piece of machinery.

I walk on past the house, cross onto the road and continue four more blocks until there is a passageway into the field. I go six rows deep into the cornfield. The unharvested corn here is six to twelve inches over my head. The corn stalks are thick. The ears are fully developed and protrude to hit me as I walk down the row. I have become invisible. I cannot see out of the field, just as no one can see in. The growth of green is too thick.

I walk back toward the eastern edge of the field staying in the row I started in. The ground under foot is lumpy and soft. I am forced to walk slowly to avoid falling. I stop five feet from the edge of the field and look at the house. The cycle is still there.

I struggle to sit, finally losing my balance and falling the last six inches. I turn so I can watch the house. Nothing is happening. I look at my watch: eight o'clock. The sun is warming the corn and it moves gently in the wind. The bees and grasshoppers are busy. I look back at the house and the cycle is gone. Damn, sun is up, it's hot. I must have fallen asleep. Eleven o'clock now. How long has the cycle been gone?

I crawl to the fence, roll under it and slowly stand. I am unable to climb over fences with my bad balance. I risk losing important stuff.

I walk toward the house. Deep grass slows me. It grabs at my feet trying to trip me. I cross the muddy driveway and walk up three steps to the porch. Gently test stepping on the thin old boards before the front door. Walk to the door, I knock loudly. If someone comes, I will be looking for a Mr. Larry Mac.

There is no answer. I knock again. Still nothing. I try the door handle, locked. It's locked but loose in the frame. Something in the settling of the house has left the door looser than it should be. I twist the handle as hard as I can, shake it back and forth, up and down. Nothing. Then I remember to push and it swings open. I walk in quietly, and shut the door. What a rush. It's my first breaking and entering. Totally surrounded by someone else's possessions. However, this dump with its sour smell kills the thrill quickly. I'm standing in the kitchen. Center of the room is a table surrounded by four chairs. Chairs are covered in red plastic but the table is so covered with dishes, pizza boxes, and other waste it's not possible to tell what color it is. Cupboards and a counter cover one wall. There is also a stove and refrigerator. I can tell that they started life as white appliances. Now they are more gray to brown with artistic slashes of dried food applied liberally. Garbage is everywhere. More pizza boxes, drink containers, beer cans and bottles, all lie strewn on the floor. Dirty dishes cover every flat surface in the kitchen. The next room has a television and an easy chair, a stand with a small lamp sits next to the chair. The stand is empty. There is a large pile of discards between the stand and the wall. It looks as if someone had just swept everything off the stand and onto the floor. One wall contains a very large Harley Davidson motorcycle poster with a half-dressed wench laying on it. Incredibly, this skank poster may be the best thing he has. I think the owner could actually be rich if he would just recycle his beer cans. Last room is the bedroom. Unmade bed, dingy sheets, clothing casually deposited everywhere.

A small bathroom is attached to the bedroom. Its smell is sufficiently pungent to keep me from going in there.

I am here in the house but can find no evidence. Nothing here to even suggest who owns it. No papers, books, drugs, nothing. Refrigerator holds rotten left over stuff with two beers unopened. In the freezer there is a short oblong piece of something unidentifiable rolled up in plastic wrap. I stick it in my pocket. It's small and I don't know what it is. Everything else I see is useless as evidence. I was so sure I would find incriminating evidence in the house. Now I am stuck. I need to get out fast and I have wasted the day. No other real leads to pursue – without more evidence – the motorcycle gang is not my problem.

I look around the kitchen one last time but see nothing to help me. I plan to leave out the rear door. Go straight back to the cornfield and return to town the way I came. On my first step, I trip over an empty food carton and grab the kitchen table for support. It moves about two inches. I pull it back to its original place. Looking at the table leg nearest me, I notice I left slide marks. My first thought is that there was something wrong with the linoleum because I did not push the table that hard. Then I see that there are many marks.

They are about three feet long. The marks all show that the table was pushed towards the rear door many times. I push the table over to the rear door. "Why is he moving this table around?" I look at the ceiling first. Has he stashed drugs and money up there? "No, that would be too stupid even for him." No one would use the table to stand on routinely.

It has to be the floor. I pick and push at the linoleum under the table. Nothing. I step back toward the sink. Study the floor hard. There is a slight bend downward near where one table leg had sat. I push at it and it moves. Now I see. The linoleum in one solid piece in the design of checkered tiles. Someone has cut along the lines of the tile design completely around the table area. I raise it and drag it completely off to one side. A trap door. I flip it up and back on itself. There is a basement under the house. I can only access it by a ladder down inside the trap door. I look down in the dark, can see nothing. I go over to the door and push all of the light switches on. I can see a light through the trap door. Without thinking too long and half paralyzed by fear, I sit on the edge, grasp the ladder and go down. I see a single bed under the large fluorescent light. It has been raised at least two feet higher than normal and it is covered with a white thin plastic pad. There are straps still attached to the legs of the bed, looking as if someone had been tied down there. There is blood on the floor around the bed. This guy likes rough games. There is a large freezer against one wall. It looks covered with a greasy film and it is chained shut. In one corner I see a small table covered with bags of white powder. There are also ten or twelve blocks of money. I grab a bag of powder, a block of money, and climb out. I quickly close the door, turn out the lights, replace the linoleum and table and leave out the back door. I walk straight back to the cornfield without looking around. Once I am in the field and invisible, I turn and look. No one is in sight. No one is following me.

I walk back eastward still in the corn until I see an opening near a city street. After that, it's an easy stroll back to Frank and Jennies' house with the drug and money hidden under my shirt. There is no one around right now, but when we talk, I will have more information for Frank to consider.

CHAPTER ELEVEN

Sheriff Thatcher's office is in the Brownstone courthouse just two blocks off Main street. The building has three stories; he is on the second floor. They finally air-conditioned the courthouse six years ago and the front wall of his office is glass now. His receptionist/telephone person is a Hispanic lady named Rosa. She is in her fifties, has four children that he knows of, she is efficient, courteous, and a resource that he depends on. Although the monthly schedule comes from Thatcher, everyone knows it's prepared by Rosa and just signed by the Sheriff. The person controlling the schedule wields the power.

The Sheriff has his own office and the other three deputies share an office with three desks. He has been on the job for twenty-two years now and is beginning to think he should retire.

Sheriff Thatcher has not had a good morning. Hell, it's been a terrible morning, a horrible week and an all-around drop kick shit month. Three deaths locally; an old man and two bikers. All three are grisly, highly visible deaths that the newspapers are continuing to slap across the face of his constituents. Three deaths in one month are upsetting but not newsworthy nor of any care to the Sheriff unless a crime is involved. But when your citizens start getting ripping apart, then the Sheriff has to do something. He is the one who has to stop it. The evening news from Sioux Falls and Sioux City has been talking about it. And Thomason, the editor of the Yankton Press and Dakotan, who had always supported him, now starts every paper with an incendiary headline. Well, he has to do something.

Now more bad news, Sheriff Sanders is reporting that two more bikers have been killed up on one of the campgrounds of Lake Tripp. He and Sanders have a good working relationship. Quite necessary as Sander's jurisdiction is just north in the next county.

Sanders also said there is an additional biker who had been wounded but he won't say how he was wounded or who did it to him. Quite plainly he was shot. But the biker is silent as a cob stuck up a dog's ass.

Somebody is turning his quiet little town into the wild west. This is going to escalate the hell out of the bad press. His deputies had not noticed anything unusual. Traffic stops and DUI's were keeping them busy. Then the one night of violence with two dead bikers,   then everything okay seemed okay for a day until the older man, John Cedrics is killed.   Now this incident at Lake Tripp. Nobody really gave a damn when those bikers got killed but when Cedrics was murdered, everyone began to take notice. He was one of them and I'm supposed to protect us.

He drives down to CHICKS BAR first to talk with Brode. He parks the car, with the large Sheriff printed on the side, in front of the bar's main entrance and walks in. He can see Brode's in a rage. Brode is letting off steam when Thacher enters the bar. He's throwing stools, bottles, tables, anything he can find. He screams at the other bikers, punches several of them, the bar, the wall, anything near him.   His rage stops immediately when he sees the Sheriff.

He confronts Sheriff Thatcher.   "What the hell do you want? Why are you not out there in your little toy car finding the bastard that did this to my people."

"That's what I am here for. Are those two who died up there and the one who got wounded up at Lake Tripp your people? "

"Yes...Yes...God Damn it. They are mine."

"What were they doing up there?"

"They were just riding. We do that here a lot. Just ride. We are a motorcycle club. How about you riding your ass around a little and catch the bastard that's doing this. "

"You are hanging your basket higher than you can reach when you talk to me that way, Brode." Sheriff Thatcher replies. "You best stop worrying about what I do and start worrying about what you do. You better start riding herd on these animals. I am telling you now, stay close, stay quiet, you and your whole gang. Do you understand? No retaliation strikes. Do you hear me? Right now you and this bunch are as popular in this county as ripe rat on a buffet table. One more incident that I follow back to you 'Servants' and I will run the whole lot of your sorry asses out of town. Now why don't you just open your mouth and tell me I can't."

Brode looks at the Sheriff, then at the gang. Blood is singing in his ears. "You best get the fuck out of here Fat Boy, before we paint the inside of the bar red with your blood. No one talks to me that way."

Thatcher is unimpressed. "You better listen. One more death and you are gone."

Sheriff Thatcher looks around deliberately looking at each biker in turn. Then walks slowly out to his car. If he can get Brode to make the gang stay quiet for a couple of weeks, it will help quiet the roar from his people.

Now off to Tripp Lake to help Sanders. If Sanders' father had not been a multi-millionaire, Sanders would be working at a MacDonalds. Enough money and power and anyone can be a Sheriff.

Thatcher could see the Tripp County official vehicles parked in single file down the campground road. Seldom is anything as depressing as a cluster of solemn officials photographing and examining evidence inside a yellow crime scene tape. Sheriff Thatcher walks over near Sheriff Sanders.

"Hey Tom, long day?"

"Come on in. John. Glad to see you could make the party. Watch your step there. I can sure use the extra eyes. This is a bad one. Got coffee and a roll there if you want, John. We have been here since dawn. Looked at it six ways from Sunday. I feel like I'm walking around picking up feathers while I'm supposed to be making chicken salad."

"Same crap down south. Just seems like no good answers. How are you figuring this went down?" John went for the coffee.

Sheriff Sanders looks at the tree with the tape still affixed to it. Then he looks out at the lake. "This is a difficult one but this is how I see it. Those members of 'Sabata's Servants' came riding into camp for some reason and attacked a lone man in a tent. The man in the tent must have been sleeping with a loaded shotgun because he shot and killed two of the bikers and blew the third guy's leg off. The strange part here is that the one biker got shot with buckshot, the other two got it with slugs. Can't think of why someone would load the gun with two types of ammo. I also don't understand why the one biker has a tourniquet on his leg. Why wasn't he just killed, also? For that matter, why did three bikers come into the campground? That alone is strange enough. Unless that tenter comes forth or the wounded biker starts talking, I don't see us going much farther with this. We'll have a lot of evidence but nothing concrete. We have picked up the shells, samples of the blood, the duct tape he used, and tried to fingerprint everything including the inside and outside of the shit house without much luck so far. That man in the tent killed two men and severely wounded a third. We need to get that bastard locked up. "

Thatcher says, "looks like you have a good handle on it, Tom. Do you mind if I look around a bit?"

"Certainly not. Help yourself."

Thatcher gets himself another cup of coffee. It warms his hands on the cool morning. He looks the whole camp over just standing where he is. He thinks the outhouse will be the obvious place to start so he walks over to it and looks inside. Then he slowly begins walking and looking at the ground. He circles the outhouse going in ever expanding circles. He always moves slowly while investigating. It is easy to overlook an important detail. He notices the footprints in the sand. Following the prints, he walks all the way to the other campground and finds where the vehicle has been parked. Then he returns to the first campground. He continues to move slowly. Not picking anything up, not taking pictures, just moving and studying the ground. Systematically he covers the entire campsite. He spends more than two hours analyzing the evidence presented by the land.

"You got any coffee left?" He asks Sheriff Sanders.

Sanders pours him another cup from is personal thermos. Thatcher tastes it and makes a face, "Christ, you got any sugar?"

Sanders starts to chuckle. "You are one demanding SOB. Here," he throws him two packs of sugar.

Thatcher stirs the sugar in. Looks at the sky for a moment while he thinks. "Tom, this is what I think I see here. My analysis is totally free and well worth the price. " I found one set of footprints leading to and from the campground over there." He points at the southern site. "I think that one shooter walked up here and stood in the lee of the shitter over there. I think there was another shooter in the tent. He was laying in there in the prone position with a fully loaded shotgun poking out the front of the tent. There was a third shooter lying hidden in the grass over there." He pointed at the place where the grass had been flattened by the man sleeping. He was probably covered with camo. So, my preliminary finding, before the forensics report, is that you had an ambush set up by three men with the express purpose of killing the 'Servants' gang members. Definitely premeditated murder. You have three dead men walking if you can find them. Hells bells, that ought to get you reelected.

You can bet hard money that the three men are from a rival gang. Maybe we got the start of a gang war over territory starting here."

Sanders looks at the ground then studies the sky for a moment. He scratches his neck absentmindedly. "Yep, yep, yep, I can always use a little help with the coming election. But the truth is I think you probably nailed it. Certainly more likely than that single tenter/shooter theory I had. Must have been two men and a woman, don't you think. The woman would have been the one to put a tourniquet on the wounded guy. But...not much in the way of forensics to help us. I doubt we can trace the tape or the shells, no other good evidence, no fingerprints, garbage, nothing. It's a very clean crime site. And what's with this damn bike burning? They do that just to get me out of bed early in the middle of the night? Unless someone comes in and confesses, I think this case will go unsolved. It looks like the murder over there in your county last week, except they used shotguns. Which doesn't help a lot. Do you know anyone in this part of the world that doesn't have at least two shotguns. There is simply no way to trace where it came from. "

"I can't see the shotguns leading anywhere," says Thatcher. "I suppose you check with the local gun shops and see if anyone just bought a new one. You could get a lead that way. How about any relatives or friends of John Cedrics? I've had inquires out but no responses. Far as anyone knows he had no truck with any of the 'Servants'. Shit, maybe it's something as simple as a drug buy gone bad."

"Well. Tom, I better get on back home. Work to do, Deputies to piss off. If you catch a break or think of anything, give me a call."

CHAPTER TWELVE

It was Jennie's day for Yankton, the closest town with a mall. Her beautician had packed up and moved to Yankton three years ago. She needed to have a larger customer base to remain in business. Now Jennie was forced to drive the thirty miles over there to get her hair done. A woman will never stop going to the beautician who does her hair right. One or two bad haircuts when she was still a teenager had taught her that firm woman's truth. Now, it's a trip to Yankton every two weeks. An additional benefit was that groceries were cheaper in the new big supermarket. She usually went to one of the three really good cafes for lunch and then out to the mall to look at some new clothes or shoes. Her best friend, Connie, usually went along and they made a day of it. Connie was stuck helping her tenth grader, Jared, complete his science project so Jennie was going alone. She had the house spruced up, her shopping lists in hand, and was on to highway 60 by ten o'clock.

Brode is still livid. No one talks to him the way the Sheriff had. He should have killed him right then. He drink two shots of Jack with a Bud, takes a quick hit of coke, but his nerves are still raging.

Brode is not tall, something he has never missed. He likes to show tall guys that height doesn't help in a fight. He is been the youngest of six kids, three brothers and two sisters. His life turned hard when his father left the house. Brode was in the second grade. Attention from his mother after that time was rare, from his siblings too common, something he tried to avoid. He had been severely pounded many times since the early days in grade school. He had never liked school, but by the second grade he was the toughest kid in class. He had his own small gang in the third grade and left school for good in the seventh grade. He quickly aligned himself with local drug dealers. He was a runner/deliverer. He proved to be reliable and soon started moving upwards in the gang. Certainly some of his rapid rise was due to his strength and willingness to fight. He had a rectangular build, almost boxlike. He was strong enough to be physically impervious to most pain. He had been cut, shot, and whipped with a chain once; still, he had never been severely injured. He usually just shrugged off pain and flesh wounds letting them heal by themselves. When he fought, he would let his opponent close in on him and hit him several times just to get close enough to hit his opponent once. One blow is generally all it took to win his fights. He never stopped with only hitting them the one time though; because they were beaten and not fighting back was no reason to stop hitting someone.

By the time he was eighteen, he was set for life, solid in his gang, doing what he loved. The easy money and easy sex were just extras. He loved the life.

When he was approached with the offer to run Tanley, he had hesitated at first, unwilling to leave his home territory but the money and power was undeniable. His sterling qualities had come to the mob's attention much earlier. He has developed the drug trade, two strip bars, and now has the two motels in full swing. His greatest attribute is certainly that he never shorted the mob their cut of the action. He always pays them first. Who knew sex and drugs would be big sellers in the Bible belt.

He fires up his sled, revs the engine, enjoying the noise, slides into gear and cruises down to the highway. He takes the bridge over to the winding Missouri river roads and hammers back to speeds of a hundred plus. The speed, the combined roar of the air flying past and the throb of the bike under him feed his life. He heads into a sharp turn, feels the pressure of the bank, the heat of the motor, and accelerates out of the curve. Maybe if he his the next corner hard enough he will be able to actually fly.

Ahead of him now, he sees an older light blue sedan. He recognizes it as Deputy Johnson's car. 'To hell with them all,' he thinks as he swing out to pass. Riding at least forty miles an hour faster than the sedan, he barely has time to lean in hard and smash his fist into the driver's side window. Glass explodes everywhere. He takes several seconds to right his bike, then sails straight on, and looking back, he sees the sedan slip over the side of the road into the ditch and flip onto the right side. He can hear a tremendous loud roar, then he realizes it was coming from inside him.

Frank is on patrol this morning. Making the county safe for the good tax-payers. So far he has given three speeding tickets and two included tickets for no seat belt. He feel like a doink giving seat belt tickets but it brings in extra federal money. He used to drive the full shift, but with the county budget and price of gas, parked surveillance is correct procedure now. He sees a plume of smoke off to the east on the highway towards Yankton. He starts his motor while he calls it in. He is on his way to investigate before the call is completed.

Sheriff Thatcher sees smoke rising in the morning sun directly ahead of him. He has been driving slowly back to Tanley, reassessing everything he has seen this morning and thinking about the resolution. Now he picks up speed. No squawk on the radio. Then he hears Deputy Johnson calling it in.

Topping a rise in the highway, Sheriff Thatcher sees a light blue sedan in the ditch on its side. There is a fire burning in the ditch; it is lapping at the rear tire trying to engulf the car in flames. He drives across the road into the ditch and stops just short of the car. He puts out the flames with his fire extinguisher, then looks into the driver's window, which, of course is now tipped up. He needs to jump to look in the broken window but he recognizes Jennie immediately. He reachs up and unlocks the door, then scrambles up the car. Opening the door as far as he can, he leans into it hard and crimps the metal so the door can not reclose. He plans on unbuckling Jennie, then pulling her out through the door on top.

Fortunately, Frank's patrol car rolls up. He comes running up. "Jump down and we'll set it back on the tires." He goes to the top of the car and lays a shoulder into it. The sheriff slides off the top and begin to push with him. They get it rocking and then shove it over back onto its wheels.

"Jennie," Frank shouts at her, "Are you okay?" She is still not moving. Her left arm is bent at a strange angle. He continues to shout at her until the ambulance arrives. By the time they have unbuckled her, her arm immobilized, she is starting to respond. They lift her onto the gurney, then strap her down and roll her to the ambulance. She is conscious now. Her face is white from the pain and shock. She begin to cry softly as they load her into the ambulance.

"I will see you at the hospital darling," he shouts. "I am right behind you."

CHAPTER THIRTEEN

I am rising from my afternoon nap when Frank comes in. He is very quiet, looking angry and tense.

"Did you hear," he says, "Jennie was in a car accident on the way to Yankton. She broke her left wrist. They kept her overnight for observation."

"Damn," I say, "glad nothing worse happened."

"Thatcher arrived at the accident before me. We pulled her from the wreck. At the hospital, she told us that a biker pulled up next to her and smashed her window with his fist. In dodging the blow and the flying glass, she drove right into the ditch."

"Does she know which biker?"

"She didn't recognize who it was. The sheriff took Brode in for questioning. Maybe he knows who did it. Probably wouldn't tell if he knew. Thatcher was still talking to him when I came home."

"Come for a ride with me," I say.

We drive his cop car past the house, turn around several blocks up the road, and then come back and park across the road from the house. No cycle was there. I ask "Whose house? Do you know?"

"That is Brode's. I think the whole gang uses it at times, but Brode owns it. I've wondered at times why it didn't cave in with all of them crowding in there, drinking beer and jumping around."

"I went in there today. I found drugs, money, and a lot of blood in the basement. I also found this." I pull out the oblong package, I found in the refrigerator, out of my cooler and show it to Frank. "I don't know what we can do with it but I had to show you." I unwrap it. A small severed finger lay in my hand.

"Damn, damn, damn, wrap it back up and keep it cool. When I go in tonight, I will see if I can fingerprint it. I think we have to include Thatcher in at this point. He may have some better ideas and I know that we will need him."

He starts up and drives off. I say, "I'm only worried that he will throw me in jail right off. It is what Sheriff's like to do right off. Throw everyone in jail then sort it out. It was hard enough opening up to you, give me some time to think about the Sheriff. You can tell him all you want, but don't tell him who I am." We pull up in front of the hospital. "Let's see how Jennie is doing."

She is in a hospital bed with her left wrist cast. Seems in a good mood considering. I think to myself 'She still looks beautiful'. She has the television on so enough noise fills the room that no one can really hear us talk. She tells us of the fear when the glass exploded, the crash, regaining consciousness in the ambulance. "Frank, it was Brode. I saw him coming in the mirror. I know it was him. We have to move out of this town. I can't take this anymore." Tears well in her eyes. I feel them forming in mine also and have to look away.

We sit keeping her company for a short time. Then drive past CHICKS INN. A party in full swing fills the bar to overflowing. Clusters of men in kerchiefs on their head and wearing their colors stand in small groups together talking. Music is blaring. Everyone holds a beer. Several lift their middle finger in a salute as we roll past.

I had been told there were twenty to twenty-five members but tonight I can easily see more than one hundred. There are at least twenty masculine looking women mixed amongst the bikers. I suspect they can do no better.

"What the hell Frank, where did they all come from?"

"Those Sons of Bitches, they called their brothers-in-arms to help celebrate running my wife off the road. Probably gangs from Sioux Falls and Sioux City."

"What do you say? Let's load up and just walk in there killing as many of them as we can. I suspect God will give us a little golden medal for each one we free from him mortal coil."

"Don't tempt me, Matt. I know you're joking, but everything in me wants to do just that."

"Give me a little time to think this out. It will not stand, Frank. This is too much shit for me to take." He stops the car and I get out.

"I'll be back later." I walk off down the street, lighting a cigar. I walk all the way to the river. Sit there watching the water. Thinking. It goes together well for me. My brain is tied to flowing water. I need to do something. Whatever happens at this point goes from the bar outward. I sit and wait for the bikers to leave. Frank might be stuck with a moral quandary but I am not. In the unofficial philosophy of the wartime Marines, "Kill them all, let God sort 'em out."

CHAPTER FOURTEEN

The sign over the bar is still lit but the parking lot is finally empty. No noise is coming through the open door. I watch until the unwashed hordes depart. I have a knife sheathed to each leg, the shorter skinning knives. I open the front door and walk boldly in. It would be too late to run, anyway, if there are bikers inside. I look around quickly, see no one there except the bartender.

"Can I get a Bud?" I drop a five on the bar.

The bartender pulls a beer from a cooler, pops it open, and slides it toward me. Then he picks up the five and shoves it in his pocket.

It's a circular bar with an opening on either side. It sits in the center of the room. There are a bunch of coolers, a shelf of glasses, and six bottles of Jack lining the top of one cooler. The overpowering smell is stale beer and cigarette smoke. The walls, the ceiling, and the floor are painted a flat black. A huge Rebel flag covers most of the right wall. Must have a southern boy here. The rest of the walls are covered with racist graffiti. My eyes are watering. I was right about the pool tables being off to the right. Other than neon signs, the florescent light over the bar is the only light.

"You a local boy?" I ask him.

"What the fuck is it to you?" he says.

I light a cigar.

"No cigar smoking. State law."

"Fuck off, my cigar makes this dump smell better. You can call the cops if you want." I take another puff on the cigar.

"I won't, but if one of the members comes in, he will probably stick that up your nose."

"Well, I will keep smoking until then."

"Unless he's in a bad mood, then he will probably kill you first, then stick it up your nose."

I try to sit on a stool. They are just crap, rickety and uneven. I'm unsure why they even are left in the bar. I stand instead. "Are you one of the a member's of this bike gang or are you just another wannabe?"

"I am neither. I'm just a bartender. I know who you are, though. They all been talking about you. You are the one they are looking for. Big score to settle."

"You want to try to settle it?"

"Like I said, not a gang member. Not mine to settle."

"Tough gig bartending to these animals?"

"As a group they're shit walking. When you get to know them individually, they are just men.

Rough men but still just men. How about taking a hike now, I'm tired of hearing you prattle on."

I hear a low rumble in the distance. "Sound advice. See you soon."

I set down my beer and walk to the back of the bar, pass by the restrooms and walk out into the night air. Fresh air with oxygen tastes great. I walk rapidly past the dumpster toward town.

My rapid walk is not as rapid as it once was. My knee replacement and peripheral neuropathology have slowed me down. Still, I am not strolling. I am moving as fast as I can. After turning several corners and traveling at least four blocks, I slow down to catch my breath. Looking back, I see someone turn the corner behind me and continue walking toward me. Damn, double damn, and rat cahones, now what?

I turn the next corner and walk in a direction away from Frank and Jennie's. Whatever happens, I have to keep them away from connecting me with them. I try to pick up speed but when I look back, he has still gained on me. Less than a block away now.

"Hey, "he hollers, "wait up, I want to ask you something."

I am walking on the right sidewalk; he is coming down the left sidewalk. He takes a right oblique and walks across the swale and out into the road, directly at me. I turn to stand facing him near a large cottonwood tree. In the dark by the side of the tree, I take out my skinning knife from its sheath on my right ankle. I have seen countless Hollywood westerns in which the ruggedly handsome star throws a knife thirty feet or farther and impales a bad guy stopping him in his track. Wow, as a youngster, I was impressed. And as a consequence, as a young man, I tried to learn to throw a knife. Hopeless. I tried ninja stars, switch blades, darts, and K-BARs. I couldn't get one to stick in a board at ten feet. My Drill Sergeant told it to me plain.

"That's all movie shit. Marines never throw their knife. It's the last weapon he has. He never lets go of it."

I take out my other skinning knife from the sheath on my left leg. I'd seen an Apache warrior demonstrate knife fighting. Probably the greatest knife fighters of all time, the Apache carried all the knives he owned into battle. He threw them rapidly, threw them hard, and was incredibly deadly. But he only threw them after he had closed with an enemy to a distance of twelve inches or less. I can throw and stick a knife twelve inches.

I hold my blades down by my side where I hope they will not be seen.

"What did you want?" I say.   Adrenalin is thundering in my ears. It is too late for flight. With my speed it never was much of an option. But I'm thinking fight is not such a great option either. This guy is too big and too fast. He's about five foot ten inches tall with the heavy shoulders of a former football player.

"Just this," he says, beginning to run the last five yards at me. He has his right arm pulled back, hand fisted up. The forward force he's built up with his body weight, running speed, and the punch he is going to throw could literally shake my brain loose inside my skull.   He must think I am into fisticuffs. He is moving toward me with a speed of at least ten miles per hour. I do that which he never expects. I step toward him and throw the knife as hard as I can. I estimate it to be traveling at roughly eighty miles an hour. It travels less than ten inches before it impacts his chest. It is a short distance and I had been holding the handle so there is no time for the knife to rotate. Therefore it is the blade that strikes him. That ninety mile an hour blow drives the blade deeply into him. He grunts loudly.   His forward movement together with the weight shift to throw the punch and the blow from the knife leaves him slightly out of control. As his swing is half completed, I ruin his plans further by dropping to the ground beneath his punch. He tries to change the direction on his swing and stop his forward movement but his speed and strength defeat him. His left foot has already caught my pelvis and I roll into the foot. His balance lost, he begins swearing as he falls over me. I rapidly thrust upwards with my knife which I have now shifted into my right hand. Luckily I catch him half-way up on the inside of his right thigh. I slash against his leg as hard as possible. I know he has been severely injured. I try to kick him further from me, then pull my knife rapidly back towards me in a slicing manner, but catch nothing.

I roll away and attempt to stand but he kicks at me with his left leg catching my left shoulder with a powerful blow as I try to roll. I flip over twice trying to disperse the force of the kick and to distance myself from him. I swing my blade wildly but connect with nothing. I can see my first knife still embedded in his chest. I pull my remaining knife closer to my body preparing for his next attack. My mission now is to stay as far away from him as I can for as long as I can. Nothing is as tiring as blood loss, and I hope he is squirting out quarts. The knife in his chest and the wound on his leg are both causing blood loss.

"What's going on there," I hear a woman shout at the same time I see a porch light go on. I hear a door slam. "I have called the police," she yells.

I am focusing on the man. I stay as far away from him as I can. Bleed, baby, bleed. I am holding my knife in front of me making circle eights to thwart his attack.

"Get lost bitch or you're next," he growls at the woman. Then totally ignoring my knife, he pushes himself off the cottonwood tree directly at me.

He lands with incredible force. I am knocked over on my back, my head slams hard into the ground. I feel the handle of my knife being pushed deeply into my chest. It feels like my breast bone is cracking. I struggle to keep the blade straight up at him. I want to move to relieve the pain, but I know the force pushing against me is also pushing against him. The blade side of my knife is biting deeply into his chest. I try to wiggle the blade inside him as far as I can.

He moans softly, exhales slowly, then lays motionless.

I am being soaked with what I hope is his blood. I try to push him off but he's too heavy. I wedge an arm under him to try and pry him off using what leverage I can gain between the ground and his body. I get nowhere; it's like pushing on a large wet sponge. His body offers no resistance. I try to rock him but without resistance it's hopeless. Then I feel him move just a small amount, and turning into the way he is moving, gets me partially free. I lay back exhausted. The woman has come to help me and is pulling on one of the dead biker's arms, and I wrestle and squirm and squeeze and finally get free.

I roll over on one side towards the woman but I am too tired and cannot stand. I sit up instead and look at her. "You saved me. I would have been stuck under that mammoth lump of cow flop until the police came if you hadn't helped. Thank God for you."

"I have called them so they should be here soon," she says. "They will be able to help you. Can I give you a hand up?"

"I could sure use it." I stretch out one hand to her. She takes it in both of hers, then gently begins to pull on me. Together we work me into a standing position. I get my first real look at my guardian angel.

She is a pretty lady dressed in jeans and a sweatshirt. Looks to be the perfect size -five foot four inches tall- and the perfect age – about ten years younger than me is my guess. Her weight is close to one hundred and fifty pounds. Yes, she is good-looking and stacked.

"I am Matt. As much as I thank you for everything, I have to go now. I need to leave before the police get here."

She looks at me a little startled. "What do you mean?"

"Well, it's like this, if the police put me in jail, the friends of that dude will kill me before morning. I think you have probably heard of the 'Servants' living here in Tanley. I would have no chance locked up without weapons."

"What can I do?" she asks.

"Just let me go. Forget what I look like. Tell the police you looked out at the fight once but stayed inside. That should keep you safe."

"You better go now," she says, "I can hear sirens. By the way, my name is Alisha."

I go back to the biker, place his hand around the knife handle. Then turn and begin walking away down the sidewalk.

"Not that way," she shouts. "Go around behind my house. The garage is open. Stay there until morning. They won't find you there."

I reverse course, walk behind her house, enter into the garage and stand there at the window at the front of her garage, watching the local police officers deal with the dead biker. The front of Alisha's house is decorated in red and blue strobe lights for more than an hour. Thankfully none of the crowd has come to look in the garage. I have opened the door to her car and climbed in to sit down. I believe it to be a late model Buick. I know it to be comfortable to an exhausted old fart.

I wait a full thirty minutes after the police have carted off the body before I leave the garage. I walk straight back away from her house. When I reach the next cross street, I orient myself and walk to Frank and Jennie's. Their house is dark, so I quietly put my clothes in plastic garbage bag, shower quickly and pass out seconds after crawling into bed.

CHAPTER FIFTEEN

Kester walked in wanting a beer.

"He just left. After him! Go! Go! Go! It's the old guy! Get him! Make him dead!" Al screamed at him, while pointing at the back door.

Kester ran out the back door in hot pursuit.

Al, the bartender, relaxed, sat back down on his stool. 'Who knows, Kester might be the one to take care of the problem. He wasn't the fastest hound in the pack, but he was strong and mean. That should count for something.'

A half an hour later, Al made a telephone call. "Ma, I want you to make a call. I think we need outside muscle for this guy. He's a greater danger than I thought. Think you can get me some help."

"I'm certain I can arrange that. I think you're right, this guy will be a problem," he heard.

The next morning in a small apartment on Western Ave. in North Chicago, a man put his matching revolvers and a silencer into his suitcase and went down to his car.

CHAPTER SIXTEEN

It's early afternoon when I get out of bed the next day. I hurt. It hurts to get out of bed, hurts to take my clothes off, hurts to climb in the shower, hurts to look at this battered black and blue body in the mirror. It even hurts to open the bottle of aspirin I find. I take six tablets hoping to reduce the swelling in my shoulders and hips. Thank God, hot water helps ease the pain. Maybe I will live. I shower long. Lots of hot water, lots of soap. Two luxuries unavailable living on the road.

I check out my clothes. I still have one pair of clean jeans. At least I haven't worn them since I bought them at Goodwill.   I find a shirt I've only worn twice and my wardrobe is complete.

After dressing, I go into the kitchen looking for Frank or Jennie. No one is home. I pour coffee from the cold half empty pot and wander into the living room. I've stayed here three nights and never seen any rooms but the kitchen, bed, and bathrooms.   One big overstuffed chair, the standard recliner and a plain looking leather couch. The couch has a lamp stand on each side and there is a free standing lamp next to each chair. Books are everywhere. There are two full bookshelves with additional volumes stacked near the chairs. There is a television in one corner and an upright piano against the far wall. I look in every room just for curiosity's sake.

Then I'm out on the street. Important things to do now, I am strolling slowly over to Alisha's place. The street looks normal this morning, all the mess from last night has been cleared away.

She lives in a small, white, two story frame house with an enclosed entryway bordered by two well-trimmed evergreens. There are mums planted across the rest of the front and they are alive with the golds of fall. There is an apple tree on the right side of her yard, heavy with fruit. Behind the tree, I see a well-tended garden with ripe, ready to pick tomatoes.

I'm a little nervous but I ring the bell, wait seconds, then ring it again. The door opens slowly, her head appears looking out, "yes," she says.

I don't think she recognizes me. "Hi, I'm Matt. We sort of met last night when you saved me. I wanted to come by and thank you again."

"Come in, Matt," she says opening the door farther. "I hardly got to see you last night and I certainly didn't expect to see you today. Would you like a cup of coffee, or maybe some tea?"

"Yes please, a little tea sounds wonderful." She leads me into a clean, well-cared-for living room with a couch and several new looking easy chairs. Near one chair on a small stand is a wicker basket with skeins of yarn and several knitting needles sticking out. Her walls are hung with what appear to be original paintings by local talent. The colors all bright and lively.

She walks through the living room into the kitchen. She is dressed in a simple light blue dress which moves nicely as she walks. I see now that her hair is a pretty mahogany brown.

Her kitchen stops me. Everything; walls, cupboards, refrigerator, even the windows is loaded with pretty things. I see needlepoint, pictures of smiling people, several framed cross stitch pieces of children and balloons, and little wooden signs with pithy sayings everywhere. Alisha obviously has a special love of hummingbirds and flowers. I see them painted everywhere. There is an apple pie cooling on the counter by an open window. Its smell is heavy on the air. The room is like an explosion of femininity. Her house has that wonderful a-woman-lives-here-fragrance that men like but can never get right.

"I love your place. What a beautiful kitchen."

"Thank you. I just finished the pie for Megan, next door, or I would offer you a piece. It's going to the church buffet on Sunday." She smiles at me. I notice again that she is very pretty. Her hair is arranged off her face, hanging down a little off her shoulders. Spectacular. I wonder if I will ever feel that hair.

She sets two fragile cups and saucers on the table. Takes a now whistling tea kettle from the stove and fills a tea pot with hot steaming water, swishes it around, then dumps the water out into the sink. She puts tea from a canister into the tea pot and refills it with hot water.

Her movements are smooth and sure, almost athletic. She has a grace that I've rarely seen and always admired. I can't remember being transfixed by a woman making tea before.

She sits caddy-corner to me, fills both cups with tea and with a graceful flourish pushes mine towards me.

I sip my tea looking at her, "Very nice tea."

"I always make it like that. I think getting the tea pot warm first helps bring out a fuller flavor. Matt, would you like to tell me about last night? That man was killed. The police are searching for his killer. Of course, we both know that's you."

"I don't know what to say to you, Alisha. I was forced into the situation, he attacked me. I was trying to get away from him."

"Why would he attack you?"

"He never said anything. See...I went into Chicks Bar and had a beer. When I left, he followed me. I dodged every way I could but just couldn't shake him. As you saw, he caught up with me just out front of your house. Without the training I received from the Marines, I would be the dead one out there."

"I've always been a fan of the Leathernecks," she says. "And I'm glad you're okay. "There was a horrible noise out there with you two. It was frightening. And when I turned on the light, what I did see right away is that he was wearing that horrible black jacket they all wear. So I thought he was part of that outlaw biker gang that is tearing our town apart. I do know that you were the good guy in that fight and I am glad I could help you. I was up all night what with the police questioning me and then worrying that one of the gang members was coming for me."

"Oh dear," I say. "I am so sorry."

"It's not your fault, Matt. It was all caused by the gang. But let's change topics and not talk about last night anymore. How about you telling me about yourself."

"Not a lot to tell. I'm a beat-up, bruised, seventy year old guy who should be smart enough not to get beat-up. I am a widower. I have been on the road traveling for six, maybe seven months now. You know how it is, time goes fast and I'm never all that sure about what day or even what month it is. So now, I'm sitting here in Tanley, South Dakota, drinking wonderful tea while looking at a very pretty lady with gorgeous hair. Tell me about you now. Are you single?"

"I've been a widow, for ten years now. My husband was born here in South Dakota, worked most of his life at the gold mine in Lead. We moved here to Tanley when he retired. I think it was the tough winter months here in the Dakota's that ended up killing him. He was stubborn, though. Never would even consider living anywhere else but South Dakota."

I am quiet for a minute. "I was raised in here in South Dakota until I left for the military. I loved the summers but never found that damn snow good for anything. When I retired, I moved to Florida. Far enough south that I don't own a snow shovel. It was too dark to see much last night, and that's a shame because I find you to be someone worth looking at a lot. I have always been a little shy, Alisha, but now I'm too old to be patient. So I'm just going to straight out ask you if you want to go to Yankton for a steak tonight?" Then I add, "with me of course."

"I would love to go, but not until you tell me what your last name is. My son would be furious if I went out with a man I just met and didn't even know his last name. Maybe he is right. Maybe I should be more cautious."

"Alisha," I say, "You knew I was the good guy last night or you wouldn't have saved me. You know I am polite enough to come back and thank you. I don't smell too bad and I have combed my hair. Also, I love your house, complemented you on that great tea, and I think you are perfectly lovely. What more could you possibly want in a man?"

She smiles and looks at me. "You could tell me that part about thinking I'm perfectly lovely again."

She has an unassuming presence. She's funny, pretty, and obviously brave. What a find.

"I think you are gorgeous, I love your hair and the fetching smile, but I should warn you, Perfectly Lovely Lady," I joke, "that I may kiss on the first date, but never have sex before the second."

She chuckles too, Then leans across the table and kisses me lightly on the mouth.

"Can you help me with something, Matt?"

"Sure, what do you need?"

"The mail was just delivered, could you please get it from the box for me? I'm expecting an important letter."

"Yep, I can sure do that." I walk out the door, leaving it open, grab the letters out of the mailbox and head back inside. I offer her the mail with a bowing flourish.

She takes the letters from my hand, drops them on the table without looking at them.

"Thanks," she says. "Now Matt, am I technically correct in saying this is now our second date?" She dazzles me with that smile and taking my hand begins backing toward a new room in her house.

I am wise enough to be quiet and follow her lead. I am going to feel that gorgeous hair.

Her bedroom is cool and dark. She leans against me at the door. Her warmth and the feel of her body pushing on mine is heavenly. She is either wearing a subtle perfume or she just smells wonderful. I am getting dizzy.

"I've been single too long, Matt. I hope you don't think I am too forward but I don't want to waste any more time. "

I am quiet for once, just kiss her slowly.

The strangeness of her mouth kisses wonderfully and the feel of her body is divine. It seems to fit perfectly against mine. Her hair is soft and smells of shampoo.

Maybe my life has really not passed me by. I notice that my fingers have developed minds of their own and are trying to unbutton her dress. Nice to see that her hands are busy unbuttoning, too. I am not an experienced sexual master. I have spent my life loving one lady with whom I was wildly in love. And I have been told that the signs and signals women give during sex can be misleading. So, I could be totally wrong here, but the moans, breathing, the bites, and the thrashing around convince me that she is as satisfied as I am.

Later, she showers first, then I follow. Dressing again I feel as shy and unsure of myself as I had the first time fifty years ago. I watch her finish dressing. She is not shy about her body. And rightfully so as her body is beautiful.

"Are you still up for dinner?" I ask.

"Certainly. Let's go over early, maybe get an ice cream cone and a bouquet of flowers. I feel like I can use some fresh flowers. Then maybe walk in the park by the river."

"Ooh Sweetie, that sounds like a perfect plan."

CHAPTER SEVENTEEN

I call Alisha early the next day, "Good morning, Beautiful, any special plans for the day?"

"Not really Matt, watered the plants, made my bed, and had been waiting for your call to bring the day to life."

"Road trip, I'm thinking of a trip up to Mitchell for an afternoon of antiquing. I hear they have a great mall building full of antiques. I am hoping you will drive because I need to rent a car. I feel bad using Frank's all the time.

"Sure I can drive. I thought you had a car, a Jeep?'

"Nope. Have a pickup back in Florida is all. If we have enough time, maybe we can take in a movie and dinner."

"Sure Matt, sounds great."

"I'm leaving now, be there in a minute."

The Buick rides great. Soft, fast, holds the road, loaded with electronics that Alisha continues to try to explain to me. I don't have a cell phone and understand little of what she says. This self-parking feature could be handy though for someone who can't drive. But this girl can drive. I watch her handle this monster like a pro. She's dressed in a blouse and black skirt both accentuate her shape. She is a true pleasure to look at.

"Nice outfit, you look great."

It turns out to be a nice afternoon. We share memories of good times, things we had once had or used to use. So many items remind us of other times and places. At the end of the day, she picks out two pretty butterfly saucers and a pin for the Leathernecks football team which I purchase for her.

It is late by now, so we go right to dinner. I suggest the local steakhouse but she wants something lighter. We settle on Marlin's. Alisha had heard they hired a new head cook who is very good. The food is freshly cooked and tasty.

Then I go to Rent-A-Wreck and get an older Taurus for two weeks. I purchase the full insurance for the first time because I don't want to be held back if I have to leave quickly.

"See you at my place," she asks?"

"I'll be right behind you. See you there." It's not until I am driving back to Tindale by myself that I begin to wonder where she had heard I had a Jeep. It is easier to think without that wonderful perfume deadening my brain cells.

She makes tea again. Still excellent. We carry the tea in and sit together on her couch.

Sitting close, cuddling, not talking much, just enjoying each other's company.

"Are you really planning on leaving in two weeks?"

"I don't know yet. If I stay longer, I will have to get my own place and my own car. I can't keep staying at my niece's I do love it here but it's a big move. You are certainly an argument for extending my stay."

"You are staying tonight, aren't you?"

"I was hoping to."

We kiss and hug, even cuddle some. It seems to me that Johnny Mathis is crooning his love songs most of the night although I know the radio was off. I watch her undress again, still spectacular. We spend much of the night playing spoons and we talk lowly of nothing much. I am beginning to see how this sweet lady could be liked too much.

She goes in to shower first in the morning. I lie in bed and watch until she finishes drying her hair. It is the male fascination with the female form. Then I, too, go in for my shower. When I come out, she is standing across the bed from me with a small pistol leveled at my chest.

"Well, good morning to you, sweetheart. "

"Better get dressed quickly, Matt."

"Why? Do you plan on shooting me here, then claim I am an intruder? Too many people saw us yesterday." I have finished dressing. Sit down on the bed to tie my shoes.

"Give me a little credit, Matt. The gang is on its way to question you. I will only shoot you if I have to."

"Oh, Alicia, I was so hoping I was wrong about you. I had to ride the string out to make sure."

"You had no idea that I was connected to the gang."

"But how else could you know about my Jeep?"

"What are you talking about?"

"You told me you thought I had a Jeep. I was hoping you had heard about it from Frank or Jenny, but I suspect that pistol in your hand means you heard about it from the gang. I guess I better be on my way."

"Aren't you forgetting about this?" She waves the pistol at me.

"Did you happen to check to see if your pistol is loaded? Can you tell if it is loaded by how heavy it is? Seems that these are essential things before you begin threatening someone with it. And by the way, hiding your gun in your bedroom lamp stand falls well below normal intellectual standards." I walk out of the bedroom, go to the front door, open it and throw the bullets out on her lawn. "Next time we meet, Sweetie, I will not be such a nice guy."

"We'll get you, you bastard," she screams. "You are a walking dead man."

Actually I am not walking. I get into the Taurus and drive away.

CHAPTER EIGHTEEN

Some days out here, there is zippo for traffic. Not much in this world is more boring than sitting in a patrol car watching nothing drive by very slowly. Even ticketing for seat belt violations was better than this. Frank played the license plate word game when parked for patrol. The letters have to be made into a word in the order they are on the plate. He was debating with himself whether windjammer could actually be a word and count for WDJ when an Illinois license went by with RSD. An easy one, 'respected', no 'resend' is shorter, a better word. Thirty minutes left on this shift. He decided to drive past Alisha's, then CHICKS, then swing by and talk to the sheriff.

Alisha has a car parked in front of her house. Frank recognizes it immediately, Illinois plates RSD. Something he should let Matt know?

CHAPTER NINETEEN

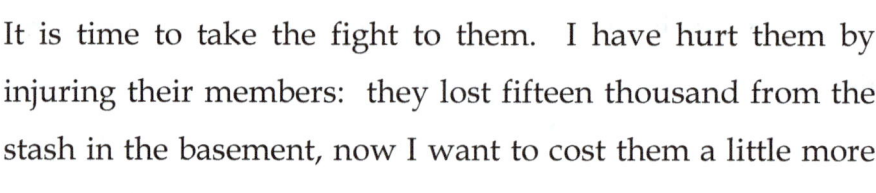

It is time to take the fight to them. I have hurt them by injuring their members: they lost fifteen thousand from the stash in the basement, now I want to cost them a little more money.

Preparation and planning. The true guide to success in any endeavor. This is basic Marine 101. If you want peace, train for war. Our Sergeant drilled it in us day and night. Prepare – Plan - Succeed. He said the Marine Corps is America's always ready warrior because without the ready warrior there can never be peace. I thought he was right at the time, I think he is still right now. Unfortunately, I also think to many of our politicians seem too make sure that we only have brief times of peace, waiting for the next war to break out somewhere. Lately, they love to say 'boots on the ground.' It's never their boots going on the ground.

One should learn from history. My history shows quite obviously that if I try to take these guys out one on one, I will soon be well dead. The absolute truth about a group of bikers is that they are stronger and faster than me. I have been lucky but luck is never a constant. Meeting them on their own ground will be fatal to me. I already have a swollen shoulder, a broken rib, a bruised pelvis, and a black and blue left wrist.

Planning and preparation...Now is the time I take the war of pain to the 'Servants.' I need a package of cigarettes with a book of matches. My kitchen matches won't do. All American class A cigarettes have Maryland tobacco in them. I buy a package of Marlboro's, they have Maryland tobacco in them. Only Maryland tobacco will keep burning when the smoker is no longer puffing. Light one, set it in an ashtray and it will burn to the edge of the ashtray. That's Maryland tobacco. My cigars may be lit but as soon as I set them down, they stop burning. No Maryland tobacco in them. This is important because I only know one booby trap and I want to use it. It's not politically correct to call them booby traps anymore, now they are called improvised exploding devises (IED) but I am going against boobs. I am not political correct.

Gasoline is one of the most powerful explosive forces readily available to everyone. The power of a quart of gas is roughly equivalent to a quarter pound stick of dynamite. Obviously, I am going to need gasoline. I love to see those bikes burning right before they explode. That afternoon I buy a five gallon plastic gas tank. I top off the gas of the

Jeep, then fill the gas can, then fill two glass one-gallon containers I have in the rear of the Jeep.

That evening in the dark, just a little after midnight, I drive down near CHICKS BAR. I park one and a half blocks away, leaving the motor running. With one of the glass jars, the pack of cigarettes, and a book of matches I walk down to the back of the bar. I light a cigarette, place it in the top of the book of matches with only the far part of the tobacco and the filter lodged against the matches. I pour the gasoline down the back of the motorcycle parked there, place the book of matches in the puddle of gasoline and leave quickly. A cigarette will not light gasoline by itself, but when it burns down to the matches, it will make the matches light. When the matches light, that gas will ignite, when the gas ignites the bike will burn, and when that bike burns, it will explode. That's what I want. With luck it may even catch the bar on fire. By the time I get to my car, I hear a very satisfying explosion. I drive out of town, heading west.

I want to drive by and see the damage but the bikers would see me and run me down.

Forty miles down the road at Burke, I stay at a motel on the far side of town. It looks and is cheap. The beds are lumpy with ancient threadbare blankets. I feel like I'm back in the service. I take a long hot shower, swallow my meds.

and a half of the bottle of Jack. Sleep the sleep of the damned. At this point, I feel like I am doing good and am winning the game against the 'Servants.'

By morning, Frank will either be with me or against me. We will see in the morning which way his heart goes.

I wake late with the cleaning girl beating on the door. "Sorry, sorry," she sings.

I go to the restaurant attached to the gas station next door for breakfast. Very nice little place with a cute waitress named Ally. I like a friendly waitress who has some heft to her. An anorexic person handling my food just makes me feel fat. Ally is about one fifty to one seventy, cute, and about fifty years old. I like her.

CHAPTER TWENTY

The house is quiet when I return. I drive into garage. The outer garage door is open, so I close it. I take off my shoes and go into the kitchen through the inner garage door. I see her immediately upon entering the kitchen. I think at first she is sleeping with her head lowered all the way forward while her body is sitting still. Both arms hang straight down. She is still dressed in the nightgown robe she wore every morning while she made breakfast and drank coffee. Her coffee cup is cold, I feel the pot, is still warm. Her eyes are open.

I walk behind her. I see a knife hilt protrude from the base of her skull. I touch her cheek with the back of my hand. She is cold. I roughly estimate her death at two to three hours. I can see that someone thrust a knife up through the back of her neck where the spine attaches to the head. It is a death stroke. It immediately stops all heart and lung functions. It turned her into an instant rag doll. That's why she is still sitting in her chair with almost no blood from the wound. Whoever killed her had training. This is not a stabbing wound that could be inflicted by luck. It also had to be someone she knew. The person who did this was a friend of her and knew exactly where to strike.

I took the fight to them, they took the fight to Jennie.

I dial 911 and ask for Sheriff Thatcher.

"Thatcher here."

"Sheriff Thatcher, my name is Matt; I am staying at the house of your Deputy Frank. I don't know the address here. I am calling to report that Frank's wife Jennie has been killed. I found her at the kitchen table when I came in this morning. I have not touched anything at the crime scene, I came right in to call you."

"I'll be right there. Touch nothing. Go sit in the living room."

Within a minute, I hear the sirens start. I am not at all sure that this is the correct action for me to take. Jennie's death has me confused. Probably should have left and let Frank handle this. He is going to have to deal with it, anyway.

Cars and ambulances pull into the driveway and line both sides of the street. Sheriff Thatcher is the first one to the door. I open it to let him in. He is followed by three people, one of whom immediately begins taking pictures of everything including me. I am instantly in everyone's way.

Sheriff Thatcher walks me into the living room, indicates a chair, "Would you please sit in here. I'll be back in a minute."

It is difficult to sit and wait. I pick up several books and try to read. I turn on the television set and then quickly turn it off. I watch one of the town cops stretch yellow crime scene tape around the front of the house. Then he stands in the driveway talking to people. Apparently he is keeping guard, making sure only authorized people can come inside.

I can see Alisha standing across the street. She is three houses up toward main street talking with a group of three other women. I know she did it. I can feel it as clearly as a testicular tazer. She did it. Something or someone convinced her that Jennie was a threat to her. So great a threat that she had to kill her.

The sheriff walks in and sits across from me. "Where were you this morning?"

"I stayed in Burke last night at one of the motels. I can't remember the name of it right off but it's on the west side of town. There are only three motels in town so you can find it easily. The cleaning girl woke me at nine, I ate breakfast at the cafe about a half a block from the motel. My waitress was named Ally, a nice lady, about fifty years old. I'm sure she will remember me. I didn't leave there until ten o'clock.

As soon as I came to town, I found Jennie and called you. Obviously I am a suspect, but I have a pretty tight alibi. And I didn't do it."

"Have you any idea who did it?" The Sheriff asked.

"My best guess would be one of the 'Servants,' but I don't think Jennie would have let one in the door. So I would think it has to be one of their friends. I am positive that Frank didn't do it."

"Frank's been on patrol. He is a friend of mine and I also believe he couldn't have done it. I will check the GPS readings from the patrol car later. But only to show he could not have done it. I better call him in and notify him. Lord, I hate this part of the job. He's been a friend for a long time."

Contemplating the reality of the situation shows quite plainly that my being in the wrong place at the right time caused all this. There is no doubt that my coming to South Dakota ended up causing Jennie's death. It was not foreseeable, but I still feel horrible. She was a sweet innocent lady, somehow caught by the unfeeling arms of a vicious enemy. I have room in my guilt basket to carry the full brunt of this. I will revenge her. This area is a kettle of crap with a fire already lit. I am raising the level of the flame. It will boil over spilling onto everyone connected to this event. I am taking the full blame for this, these people have all just let their garbage pile up and now they may be surprised when I take their garbage out.

Two hours further down the road, the body has been removed, Frank has been notified, questioned, and is now in his room. Even the yellow tape has been removed. I have made a pot of coffee, and now I bang on his bedroom door.

"Come out, have some coffee with me. We need to talk." I get the half bottle of Jack out of the cupboard. Then reconsider and bring the full one, too.

Several minutes later, he drags himself out and sits at the table. He is gray around the edges looking like he picked up ten years of age this morning. I pour him some coffee. Put a shot of Jack in it. "This will help, believe me, if it don't kill you first."

He pushes it away, I push it back, take a shot myself, swallow it, gasp and take a drink of coffee. "Let's go bucko, get that fucker down. Mourning time is over, we got work to do."

He kicks it back finally. Has more coffee. I pour the Jack in a glass this time. Put it in front of him. "Life just sucks sometimes. This is one of them times. I gotta know though, are you with me or you going to dress in black and hide for the next six months?"

"Okay, damn it," He drinks the glass of Jack. "I'm back. Let's get the person who killed her. I am with you."

"Well, Mr. Professional Investigator, who killed her? You know the town and her better than anyone else. Who did it?"

"Well, I know it was not any of the 'Servants. She would not have let them in and there is no evidence of forced entry. I think it has to be a woman. There are only three men in the world who she would have let in while in her robe, and her father is out of state, you were in Burke, and I was working," says Frank.

I reply, "That's the way I figure it too. Now the hard part, since we know it's a woman, which one?"

"I know Connie comes over for coffee, Jennie wouldn't have dressed for her. But I can't think of any reason that Connie would hurt her. She had several lady friends at church and probably several of the women she got to know through Jack at school. I can't narrow it down any more than that right now. I would say we probably have a list of about six people," says Frank.

"I did not tell the sheriff any of the obvious things the evidence points out, but this is what I have concluded. The person had to be a friend with a strong purpose behind the attack. There was no robbery and the person did not appear to be angry at Jennie-no pain or torture. Sex does not seem to play a part in it. So the reason she was killed was to punish either you or me or both of us. So, for that reason I cross Connie and the friends she met through Jack off the list. Most of the ladies at church do not have a reason to harm either you or me. So, for that reason I cross all but one of them off the list."

"Do you know who did it, Matt?"

"Well, I have a few pieces of evidence, clues if you will, that might help. First of all, the woman who I think did it, goes to Jennie's church. The woman, knew that I was staying here. She knew I have a Jeep, although I never told her I had a Jeep. She was standing on the corner this morning watching what was happening, and the final clue, she tried to kill me two days ago. I don't want my clues to be overly subtle, but take a guess who I think killed Jennie?"

"Alisha tried to kill you!! How? Why? "

"She had a pistol aimed at me when I got out of the shower. I was suspicious when she mentioned the Jeep she should not have known about. So, I removed the bullets from her gun while she was showering. She did pull the trigger, Frank, so we can be sure she is capable of murder. I don't know the reason why for sure. I believe her son is the bartender in CHICKS. I also believe he has a role in running the gang.   You should be able to find out through your office if he is her son."

"Give me a minute to think.   Yesterday, Alisha had a visitor from Chicago. Driving a light brown SUV, license plate RSD. If Alisha is involved in this, and I believe she is, after what you told me, I can see Jennie letting her and a friend in. While Alisha talks to her, the friend could have stabbed Jennie from the back. I have been trying to think of anyone who would be that good with a knife and have come up with no one. Now, I think she's hired a pro."

"Damn, that would complicate everything. But it sounds like you're right."

"Now what, Matt? I know there is something I have to do. I would sure like your help with it."

"You have my help for sure, Frank. You and I are going to kill the fiend that killed our beloved Jennie. My first thought is that, you could ask the people on both sides of the street if they saw her and a friend come here this morning. Maybe someone can put her at the scene. You could ask her if she has an alibi. You could develop all the evidence in the world against her. Even prove that the knife is hers and you know what? She will still walk free. If you could get a jury to convict her, which is doubtful, the judge would give her less than ten years and she would walk in three at the most. So here's what I think you and I have to do to get her justice,

Frank. Find out if Alisha has hired a professional. Get dressed, go over and talk to her now. A professional will not hit you being a law man," I said.

"I will be ready in five minutes. Have to get the whiskey off my breath." He was back in about fifteen minutes. "Any suggestions?"

"I think you will get a read on her just by being there. You have known her for at least five years and she just helped kill your wife. She should be pretty nervous. Ask her about the guy. Ask her why she came over to see Jennie this morning. If all else fails, tell her I'm pressing charges for attempted murder and arrest her. I will go down and swear out a warrant if I need to."

When Frank returned, we had our answer. "She swears she didn't come over to our house yesterday and that Jennie was a dear friend. She claims the car belongs to a cousin visiting from Chicago, but I ain't buying that crap. She was guarded and nervous. She is involved in Jennie's death and he is a pro; you can count on it."

While he was talking to Alisha, I had packed up all my stuff, except for the whiskey. I still have the best part of a case in the Jeep, anyway. I also have that fifteen thousand dollar block of money I took from Brode's. I packed everything in the Jeep.

"Why did you pack up?"

"We need to work separate for a bit. If I stay here they will know where I am. You are going to have to do the law stuff while I do all the illegal stuff. We need some phones. Can you get us two throw-aways? Leave your garage open today so they know I am gone. I will meet you tomorrow morning. I'll be here about ten. Okay?"

"Okay," he says, "but it sounds like you are doing all the fun stuff."

"The noise you hear late tonight will be me going for the professional. If I don't get him and he gets me, I'm counting on you to bury his ass."

I leave Tanley and head straight south. I need to find some place where I will be anonymous for a short time. Rest and get ready, that's what I'm thinking. I think the pro is staying with Alisha and I need to flush him out. I cross the bridge at Springfield and go into Nebraska. At Niobrara they have built a new Indian Casino. I figure that is about as safe as I can get. No one ever notices people at a casino. I get a room in the new motel attached to the casino.

CHAPTER TWENTY-ONE

The man was quiet and ordinary looking. Five foot ten inches tall, he was the type of person you walk past every day and never notice. He wore a seed-corn cap, jeans worn light blue with age, and a tee shirt from Disney. All standard everyday clothes meant to go unnoticed. He hated these small towns with no space to blend in. He had driven to the bar first. It had not opened yet, so he called in to his office and found the woman's address. He went to her house. He did not like meeting people but she had a significant history and could be trusted.

She hadn't known where the target was right then, but she had an additional job for him if he wanted it that morning. He had helped her and earned the extra five large. Still, it puts people on alert. Police would be moving around interviewing people. Already a deputy had come to the woman's place to interview her. He had stayed in a bedroom, an additional humiliation. If they suspected her, the problem would have escalating difficulties. Worse, she had been unable to locate the target. All he knew was that his target was an older guy driving a Jeep. He decided to leave town for a while until things cooled down. He would call her in the morning to see if she had found the target.

Picking direction at random, he drove straight south. Crossed a bridge at a town named Springfield, and had gone into Nebraska. The first place he ran into was a new looking Casino with an attached motel. He decided to stay there. He was at least forty miles from Tanley. Plus being in a casino enhances your invisibility. No one every notices anyone at a casino.

CHAPTER TWENTY-TWO

Sheriff Thatcher was looking at Pinkie. His name for the finger. It looked like the small finger on a tiny person, harvested from the left hand. He was unsure what to do with it. It had been obtained illegally, according to Deputy Frank, so it couldn't be used as evidence in a trial. He was sure Frank had not committed the illegal act to obtain the finger, but he refused to say who had.

He had it in a jar on his desk. Dr. Sayer, at the hospital, had assured him that the fixative would not break down the fingerprint or the DNA for at least ten years. Not that it really mattered because the print had come back negative and he had no one to compare the DNA to. Sayer had estimated the finger to have been cut off within the last three months. However, it had been frozen with no tissue break down so it could have been up to six months. There were simply too many missing people to compare DNA.

What was driving him crazy is why a finger. Could it have been an accident? But why save an accidentally severed finger. Could have been punishment. Maybe someone had cut it off because they were wronged. A fight? A show of loyalty? Just no way to know.

Personnel were short right now. Frank was on leave after his wife's death. Anders, the new guy was out on patrol, still called him the new guy after two years. He was okay for traffic but frequently had to have other duties spelled out. Also, he was mouthy and arrogant. Complaints were piling up from unhappy citizens. It was always his attitude and laziness when he was off duty. Thatcher thought that the trouble mostly originated from Ander's wife. Rumors of unrest there.

His third deputy, Spranger, had been with the department for twenty plus years. He was looking at retirement in the next ten years. Certainly he was an adequate deputy but he was never going to be a shining star. He was more interested in the donut shop he had started with his wife. Despite all the jokes he received because of it, it was still a good shop with great coffee and pastries. Spranger preferred to work the late shift or to be on call overnight. He wanted his days free.

Jennie's death was the question. He believed the answer would clear up the violence recently exploding in the county. The people were unhappy and after twenty-two years, Thatcher didn't want to look for a new job. The accident, the hospitalization, then her murder at home the day after her release was too coincidental. Everything was connected. That was the answer, now he had to find the connection.

Thatcher began at the neighbor on the same side of the street, just to the north of Frank's house. Pretty standard questions to everyone. What did you see this morning? Anybody out walking around the neighborhood? Did you see anyone visit with the Johnsons? Any reason you know that someone would attack Mrs. Johnson? Well, thank you anyway. Please call me if you think of something. He went up the three houses on that side of the street, crossed to the other side and came down the six houses on that side. He finished off the last two houses to the south of the Johnsons. Nothing. Well, not one positive answer to the questions. But there was something. A feeling was there that the people had been frightened.

There is always a little black and white fever making the citizens nervous, but today there was more like an undercurrent. All the answers were too much the same. No one had to think before answering. The people were just not acting naturally to him. No one doing yard work, or going shopping, or out walking for exercise. Not reasonable. He knew two of the men who lived on the street, had bowled with both of them on a winter league and had golfed with one last summer. Yet neither had bothered to come to the door to say hi. There was the smell of fear on this street. Whoever was applying pressure was using a heavy hand.

He drove back out to the accident site. The furrow ripped into the sod was already beginning to heal with new grass sprouting. The burn marks were still clearly evident. It appeared to him that the fire was caused by the catalytic converter. He had seen the older models start grass fires previously. Still something had caused the accident. Jennie had a good driving record. He doubted that she had fallen asleep that early in the morning or had just driven off the road. That did happen occasionally. He needed to check to make sure she wasn't taking any new medications. He remembered that the tires were okay when they tipped the car back upright. He walked back up the ditch reading the evidence every accident provides. Thirty yards up from the where the car flipped, he saw the broken glass on the roadway. The window had been smashed in.

He tried to remember. It was the driver's side window. Something had hit the window hard enough to shatter the window, but had not struck her. A projectile fired at her? Was the accident an attempt to kill her that he had not noticed at the time? It was time to start applying pressure on the 'Servants.'

He called Anders. "How you doing out there?"

"Flat dead today, boss. Nothing moving."

"I got some grunt work for you. I want you to head over to the dump and look through the recent trash. I'm looking for large black plastic bags that have been personally dumped. Do not bother looking through anything dumped by the Waste Management or any packed garbage."

"Damn, Thatcher, you always give me the cherry jobs."

"I want you to look in the bags. Any bag filled with empty ammonia jars, empty gallon alcohol bottles, or empty packages of cold medicine, bring them to me."

Thatcher drove over to Clabers garage where the sedan was parked waiting for the insurance inspection. He had been right, the driver's side window was smashed. No other glass was broken. There were no holes in the headliner. He checked the front seat, back seat, dashboard, nothing. No signs that a projectile had been fired into the car other than the driver's window. Perhaps it was a glancing blow that hit the glass and ricocheted away. He was stuck with a ton of good evidence and none of it pointed any clear way. Time for lunch.

He parked in the Nook's lot next to his deputy Anders's car. Sat in the booth across from him.

"How's the special today?"

"Not too bad. Plenty filling for the buck. Do I smell like I spent the morning at the dump?"

"You smell better if anything. Did you find anything?"

"I did. One bag was filled with empty Sudafed boxes and an ammonia bottle. I have the bag in my trunk, will toss it into your back seat when I leave. "

"Thanks for doing that. It was an unpleasant job that had to be done. Back to patrolling this afternoon. If you want to shower and change clothes, I understand. I'm afraid they could locate you by nose, long before they see you."

The waitress set a cup of coffee and a chicken Philly sandwich with fries before him. "Here you go, John"

"Maybe I wanted something else, Carol."

"Eat your special and keep your lip to yourself, John. The ketchup is right there." She pointed to a half full bottle. "If you need more, just come up and get it. Maybe I wanted something else indeed. Fifteen years I worked here and he's never ordered anything but the special. I swear I don't know what gets in him some times."

'We have got to take care of Jennie's death first,' he thought, 'I got to get a hold of Frank.'

CHAPTER TWENTY-THREE

This room is as every new motel room is;   bland colors, horrible simplistic prints on the walls, new carpet and a great shower. I wake slowly reveling in the luxury of the safety. I have decided during the night that I have been approaching this problem from the wrong view point. It all started with me being frightened. Then the anger took over and I felt I had to get revenge. Now Jennie's death and I have felt myself stiffen with the hard steel of resolve. Fear and anger were two fortifying emotions; now I am going to destroy this blight on the countryside.

I walk across the highway to a small cafe. Order up my favorite breakfast, two eggs over easy, grits, sausage, and whole wheat toast. And of course, cups of hot coffee. What I get is two well-done eggs, hash browns, sausage, and white toast. 'Close enough,' I think, because the coffee is great and this waitress is keeping my cup full while she carries on a light meaningless banter with me. I cover everything with a light layer of hot sauce and it slides right down.   It was great for only six bucks and a couple more for the tip. "At least you didn't cover everything with ketchup," the waitress says. "You wouldn't believe how many of these red-neck yokels cover everything with red-eye."

I am sure the Rabbit-hunter and Alisha have talked to Brode. He knows my description; he knows I drive a Jeep, and he knows about the Rent-a-Wreck. He should also know that I am coming to get him, but I doubt he takes my warning seriously.

I will not be able to go back to the rental car. They will have it booby-trapped or will be waiting for me. Either one is deadly to me. I know I have hurt them with four dead and one disabled. Also, I have told Frank about Alisha, so the county may know about her or he may have just kept the knowledge to us two. I have to count on Frank to help me or I will be lost. He and I are taking separate paths together. I don't wish to put him in further danger from the gang or from local or state law. I know I can rely on him but still I need a new base.

I am finishing my last cup of coffee. Thinking about Tanley, when I look out at the cars in the parking lot. A light brown SUV is right in front of my window. An Illinois license plate starting with RSD.

Well, well, well, is this a coincidence. It could be a completely unrelated vehicle passing through. I don't believe in circumstance. I needed to stay someplace about fifty miles where no one would find me. I suspect Mr. Hit man needed the same.

My Jeep is parked over in front of the casino. I look the same as most of the people at the casino. No reason for him to pick me out. I look around casually. Three people eating breakfast. There is a couple in the booth next to me. They are discussing the husband action from the night before. Apparently, he spent a little too much money on slots. He certainly did not have to tip that drink girl six dollars.

In the far booth, a man sits with his back to me, a shorter to medium size man with a green seed corn hat on his head. He may be my guy. Not much I can do in here.

"Hey Sweetheart, could I get one more cup of coffee, please?" I say as I pull a twenty out of my billfold. When she comes over, I give her the twenty "keep the change, Darling. Those slots were good to me last night." I ask the couple next to me, "Mind If I get yours also. It's seldom I come out with any ready cash."

"That would be very generous, thank you."

"How about you Mister, there in the green hat? Mind if I pay your bill?" I ask.

He turns a little toward me, dismisses me and says, "No thanks. I'll handle it."

I have taken my skinning knife out and laid it on the table amongst my silverware by the dirty plate. It is not a large knife, with a three inch blade, but it is sharp enough to split a frog hair into quarters. I go up and pay for the other breakfasts at the cash register, then walk back toward the door. Stretching my arms and yawning as I go. As I go past him, I pivot on my left foot and smash my right fist as hard as I can into his neck. His head bounces off the plate glass window and he appears stunned. I step back, pick up my knife and as he leans forward to stand, I hold the knife at his throat.

"How about just sitting quietly for a minute?" I ask him. He sits down immediately.

The other couple begins to stand. I tell them to sit back down and they won't get hurt. I motion for the waitress to sit with them. "I won't be long, just need some names from this guy."

He begins whining and moaning. "Please don't rob me, Mister."

"You can stop the act right now." I say. "I want information and if you don't talk, I will leave your body here."

He stops making noise and sits quietly.

"Who hired you?"

"I don't know names; I get my assignment from a telephone bank in Chicago."

My knife goes into his throat about an eighth of an inch. Blood begins running down onto his shirt.

"Want to try again?" I ask.

"I don't know her name now. I knew her as Janet Sudacao, fifteen years ago. Her husband was in with some crime figures in Southern Illinois. This call came out of the blue for me, I thought she had been killed when I got it."

"How much you getting paid?" I ask.

"Five thousand."

"You still want to try to collect it?"

"Do I have a choice?"

"Sure you do, You can pack up your stuff and get on the road back to Chicago," I say. "No need to die here. And next time I meet you, you will die. Now put your feet up on the booth. He puts both feet up. I take a small pistol out of the holster on his right ankle.

"Now give me your keys." He digs out his car keys.

"Wait here until I leave. Your car will be parked on the other side of the casino."

I leave the diner, unlock his car, and drive back to where my Jeep is parked behind the casino. He is still just sitting there in the diner with his feet up when I left. I feel he may be just a bit unhappy with me.

I put his suitcase into the Jeep, lock the SUV, flatten the tires and drive away in the Jeep.

CHAPTER TWENTY-FOUR

What the gang doesn't know yet is my resolve. They have assumed that if they made it too difficult for me to stay I would leave the area. Brode has been thinking that everything would return to normal if they could drive me away. Thus Jennie's death was an attack by the gang telling me that if I mess with them, they will hit back harder, if not to me, to others who are vulnerable. Now, it will look like I am gone since I am no longer at Frank's.

I get to Frank's house later than I wanted due to the incident at the restaurant, but he is still there. I drive into the garage and shut the door. Then I walk into the kitchen. Just a little anxious to see if he will like my new tack.

"I talked to the hit man. I have his stuff in the Jeep, shall we look through it?"

I bring in his suitcase and the brown paper bag he had in the SUV. Of course, we both like the pistols. They are sweet. US Arms Colt forty five single action beauties. They are immaculate. We split the five thousand dollars that he has wrapped up.

"Looks like he wanted to buy me a car."

Frank gives me a phone. I think we are ready.

"Frank, I am going to shower and wait here until dark if that's okay with you."

"Certainly, and anytime, Matt, my house is your house."

My attack parameter has added variables. I am going to start hurting them where they are most vulnerable. I didn't like them before, now that they hired a hit man to take me out, I am even more irritated with them. I will attack their money supply. I know the life blood of the gang is the money. The bricks of money and the bag of cocaine has to have hurt them. I consider for a time that I should once again go after the money and drug stash in Brode's basement but that theft would only prove a temporary solution as the machine producing the money is still working. I need to attack the money machine itself. If I can slow down or stop the money production, I can destroy this blight.

The biker gang, the strip bars, and the drug trade are all supported by the weakness of the general population. There are and will always be those people who feel they need more out of life. A good spouse, a good job, great kids, and health would seem to be the goal of a person's life. And yet, where are the good men and women who don't feel they are missing out on something. It seems everyone wants to throw the dice at least once. I believe it's rooted in aging.

Aging and the perception of that which they feel they have missed out on. Perhaps they could have been happy if they had only married that cheerleader with the big tits or the star of the football team. Is there a pill or surgery which would bring back my youth? Let's spend some money and see. I suppose I should have more sympathy for them, the weak and those who prey on them. But it is these people who helped kill Jennie.

I know the gang has two strip clubs, but Frank has only told me the location of one of them. That's the one I will attack first. The drive to Lester takes about twenty minutes using back gravel roads. I must of necessity drive slow. Tractors and farm machinery use these roads frequently, and especially now during the harvest season, the farmers are busy well into the dark. Headlights on farm machinery were a great leap forward in wearing out farmers at a younger age. It's dark out now and getting colder every day. Several more months and snow will cover this area.

The gravel road I was on comes into Lester from the northwest corner of town. There are few houses, thirty or less is my rapid guess. There are few street lamps in any of the neighborhoods. The brightest place in town is the open convenience store. I take a left onto Main Street at the corner by the convenience store. Main Street is only two blocks long. Buildings line the street on the left side. Only one building, a drab brown looking motel is on the right side. It seems to be fighting the weeds and scrub trees for room. All but one of the buildings on the left side are boarded up.

Cody's Place is open for business. The neon beer signs in the window indicate it to be a bar. There are six cars parked in front of the bar, two cars parked in front of the motel. I stop at and enter the convenience store which acts as Lesters' gas station, grocery store, package liquor, and tobacco shop. Pausing in front of the convenience store's security cameras, I wave and smile. They need to know who is doing this. Of course, I understand there is a better than even bet that the camera is a sham, but maybe it's real and I can irritate Brode even more. I buy a six pack of cheap beer and three packages of the small cigarillo cigars. I want matches, but they sell lighters so they don't give matches away. Cheap bastards try to work everything for an extra nickel. I have to go to the grocery section and buy the larger wooden kitchen matches. They don't ven sell the boxes of book matches. I go outside, light up a cigar and open a beer. Good evening, Lester. I hope you citizens appreciate what I am going to do to your town tonight. Something you should have done years ago. Not much but the bar keeping this town alive. If they had fought for it though maybe it would be a thriving town with pride and substance. As it is now, the bar won't let anything else get started.

I park the Jeep on an unlit street two blocks from Cody's. I am armed with the U.S. Arms Colt 45 which I carry in a concealed carry holster under my jacket. It feels like a small cannon. I also have my K-BAR sheathed to my right shin. I carry it there because I can bend to the right much easier. The surgeons told me that the prosthesis in my left knee would be great for bending, but it didn't quite work out that way. I have a good dozen matches in my jacket pocket for later.

I walk back toward town. Cool enough now to just see my breath when I exhale. Finish my cigar and litter the town road with the butt. There are currently two cars sitting in front of the motel. Six cars are parked in front of the bar. My rough calculation is eight to twelve men spending money, can't figure there are too many women spending money here in these dives. The whole place looks so cheap and dirty, I find it hard to believe men would go in either place.

I take out the K-BAR and flatten all eight tires on the two cars in front of the motel. Cross the street and stand in the walk way between two abandon buildings. I wait two or three minutes, just watching to see if anything moves, but see no action anywhere.

Just as I start out, a man comes out of Cody's, lights a cigarette, searches in his pockets for his keys, looks around for a minute, tosses the cigarette on the road, gets in his car and leaves. He is lucky. Five more minutes and he would have been walking or waiting for his car to be fixed.

I go to the cars in front of the bar, flatten all four tires on three of the cars, put my knife back in the sheath on my leg and walk as quickly as I can back to the Jeep. I still hear and see nothing. Clean getaway in progress. I drive out of town the same way I came gradually working my way south to the highway near the campground where I camped the first night in South Dakota. I pull into Sam Kelley's abandoned farm. I doubt the 'Servants' will ever look for me here.

I drive around to the back of the house. Back the Jeep as far into the trees as I can and walk out toward the house. The Jeep is well hidden by the low hanging branches of the cottonwood trees.

I tear the boards off a rear window, break the glass and carefully remove all the jagged glass. No need for a vasectomy now. I use the pen light to look inside. It looks like an empty living room. I step in and go to the rear door and unlock it. Open it and kick the boards away. Time to see what's in here. There is a kitchen to the left, a bed room to the right, and a stairway leading up to the second floor. I walk up carefully but the stairs seem sound. Two more bedrooms, one to either side and a window looking out on the porch roof right at the top of the stairs. This will all work nicely.

I bring all my gear inside, even my guns. I put the guns on a kitchen counter, check to make sure all are loaded and have a round in the chamber. I wrap myself in a blanket, lay on the tent, and within ten minutes of starting to plan, I am fast asleep.

The military had taught me and several million other soldiers to fall asleep rapidly and in almost any place. They specialize in hurry up, now wait. We could be waiting for helicopters to return for deployment to a hot landing zone and half of us would be asleep. The other half seemed to always have a deck of cards and a game of Liars Poker going. Sanity among those going into dire danger can be difficult to explain.

CHAPTER TWENTY-FIVE

The man in the green seed-corn cap walked back over to his room at the casino. He put through a call to Chicago, then laid on his bed with his eyes open, waiting. He had his call returned in fifteen minutes. Talked to the people for a short while. "I will be here. Bring everything I need to me here, tomorrow afternoon at the latest."

He laid back down again and closed his eyes. As if some cow town yokel was going to get a shake on him. 'There is unpleasantness ahead for that old dude,' he thought.

CHAPTER TWENTY-SIX

Alisha is worried. For six years she has lived here with no problems. No one ever suspected her. Lots of friends, she even sings in the church choir. Now Matt knows. Damn, if he knows, who else will know? If she had only killed him when he was still under Kester and unable to move. Or if the gang had gotten there fast enough when he was in the shower. Why hadn't she checked that pistol?

Now Thatcher is talking to people. Deputy Johnson is out interviewing people. Had anyone seen her and the quiet man walk down to Jennie's that morning? They had gone to take care of Matt, but Jennie was an excellent target of opportunity. A very real message sent to Matt and the whole town.

Al, her son, had been irritated when she had told him. He said, "I called you about getting Matt, not Jennie. Let the gang take care of gang business." Whose business was the gang taking care of if not her's and Al's. Sometimes he could be a brick.

Maybe it is time to go. Pack up and move – a new place without the threat could be a smart move. She has more than enough money. The fifty large that Brode has just given her is icing on her cupcake. Time for Al to start a legit business. Maybe a bar in a college town.

She puts in a call to Al. "I've been questioned by Sheriff Thatcher and Deputy Johnson. I think I might have to leave. If I go, you know where to find me."

Alisha pulls out her travel bag and packs up everything she needs; her papers, a change of clothes, stocks, bonds, and cash. Everything else she can replace when she goes to her new town.

CHAPTER TWENTY-SEVEN

I wake up just before one o'clock. I use my penlight to check the Nagant, fully loaded and shell in chamber; Benelli, fully loaded, shell in chamber;   U.S. Arm Colt 45, fully loaded shell in chamber. If it is not loaded and ready, why carry it. No enemy will stop while I reload.   Taking only the weapons and leaving the door open, I drive the Jeep straight back to Lester by the highway this time. I drive up through Main street, circle and head back down. Nothing moving in town tonight. Bet there was some unhappiness two hours ago. Then I drive the alley behind Cody's Bar.

The alley runs close to the buildings. Lots of trees off to the right. I can't see any buildings or lights off that way. About half way up the alley, I see that one building is indented about twenty feet. There is a light bulb hanging over a door. There is a beautiful Harley Davidson Easy Glide sitting there by the rear entrance light. I get out, leave the Jeep running, walk up to the bike, punch a good size hole in the gas tank with my knife and go back to the Jeep. I drive around to the front of the bar, roll down my window and put four rounds from the Sig Sauer through the front door. I drive to the end of Main Street and wait until I hear the roar of the Harley. I drive out of town as fast as I can down the main highway. I see the head lamp hit the road behind me and begin closing the distance between us. This could be closer than I wanted. I got the Jeep topped out and have gone about two miles when I see the cycle start to back off. I turn and head back.

I stop about two blocks from the stalled bike. I can see the rider in the head lamp trying to get his bike started. He is a short man with long hair. I drive up until I am one hundred yards away. I get out, lay across the hood of the car with my Nagant and wait until the man stands still. He is watching me, I hear him shout and wave his arms. He pulls a pistol out and fires at me. As if he could hit something at one hundred yards.

I gently squeeze the trigger of the Nagant. One of the 7.62 round cuts briskly through the air until it enters his left kneecap. It is a small bullet. It enlarges rapidly, tearing out most of the back of his knee. He is smashed back into the bike, and they both crash on over to the left side.

I drive up to look at him. He seems unconscious. Pulling out the 45, just in case, I walk up to him. I can see his left leg is shattered. I grab his right leg and pull him out in front of the bike so I can see. I wrap duct tape around the shattered knee, it takes six wraps before the bleeding slows. Throw a couple of wraps around his wrists, also. Then tape his wrists to his leg so it forces him into a sitting position. Duct tape is great stuff, fast, easy to use, and sticks to anything. I hit him a few times lightly on the head with the barrel of the 45. "Wake up." I see this guy has 'Executioner' written on the front of his jacket. "Hey. Hey." I holler at him, "You a friend of Hardin?"

"You mongrel bastard, we will castrate you before we kill you." He's awake.

"That may be, Stupid-one, but I'm betting you won't be one of them when they do get me. Now I want you to say 'hi' to Brode for me, tell him I am coming for him. You think you can remember that?"

"Fuck you."

I pull out my knife and cut off his left ear. Hold it to my mouth and holler, "Can you hear me now?"

"I hear you. Going to kill you slow."

I get back in the Jeep, reload the pistol and my rifle. Drive back to Lester and park in front of the bar. Stroll in, casually, sit at the main bar, and look around. Stinky dirty place smelly of sweat and pent-up desire. The whole inside is painted black. There is a small stage with a cloth backdrop on one wall. Four tired looking girls sit around a table near the stage. An older man walks over. I say, "Long neck beer."

He reaches into a cooler, opens the beer on the front of the cooler and slides it to me. Glass?" He asks. The music starts and two of the girls stand and start for the stage, shedding clothing as they walk. "I'm not here for the girls, I am here to talk to you."

"Yah, whatcha need?"

"I'm the old dude they are looking for, here to give you advice. Find a new job. Quit here today and don't come back. Next time I come here I won't be such a nice guy. Right now though, you better go help that biker lying on the highway. Seems he had a bad accident. He met up with some old geezer who didn't like bikers."

"Do you really think you are that scary? I've seen a ton of tougher guys than you come through those doors."

"You are probably right. But I'm the tough guy you got to deal with right now." I take a drink of beer. Light a cigar.

"No cigars in here. House rules."

"Man, everyone hates my cigars. Why are you still here?" I can see him leaning to one side and looking around.

"Girls, now would be a good time for you to leave. At least, move away from right behind me. I think this dumb turd here is going to try for that scatter gun under the bar. If

I don't drop him with my first three bullets, he may get a shot off."

The bartender stands up straight, takes off his apron, and walks out the back door. I decide not to wait to see what the girls do.

CHAPTER TWENTY-EIGHT

Sometimes good things happen for bad reasons. I am back at Kelley's farm house. My gear is inside the abandoned farm house, out of the Jeep. I have reloaded all my weapons. I want to relax and smoke. No place to sit in here other than the floor or stairway. So I go upstairs, step through the window onto the porch roof. There I lean against a wall, dangle my feet over the edge, and light a cigar. Sweet. I close my eyes and rest. Been a long day with a lot of tension. Take another puff, these things are going to end up killing me. I am wondering why I am needed here. Why do I choose to do what I am doing. There are many stalwart citizens here in the Midwest. This is the stiff-necked bible belt of the country. Why do they sit around watching the wrong element arise? If they had one John Wayne or Randolph Scott amongst them, they would have rallied the faithful and good and wiped out the evil doers. We all know what's right. Why so much dithering around?

Jennie has been killed. Jennie and Frank's son, Jack has been killed. They were killed by easily identifiable bad guys. Why do the good guys always have a reason they can't do the obvious.

I puff again. I notice a car slow down and stop near the driveway. I hear a car door open, then several minutes later I hear a car door slam. Someone knows where I am. I review everyone that it can be. I eliminate everyone but the bartender from Lester. I forgot to ask him his name. He must have followed me out of town and checked the driveways along the way to see if he could locate me. Smart little shit. I should have put a bullet in him to slow him down. I now include him in my lists as an active enemy.

A wise man can take a hint. I have been found. Will they come tonight? It's after three o'clock in the morning. Maybe they will wait until tomorrow when they can round up more of them. Better assume the worst. At best, if I hurry I can prepare a reception for them. I calculate thirty to forty-five minutes before they are back.

I take all my camping gear and extra clothes and put them in the upstairs master bedroom closet with the block of money, the Glock, and the whiskey I have left. If I make it back, I will need money, a weapon, and a drink.

I check the shotguns and rifle again. They are loaded, shells in all the chambers. Carry all my weapons to the Jeep. Long guns in the front seat, butts on floor and barrels pointed at roof. Knife strapped to right leg. Pistols all lying on the front seat. I drive the Jeep up through the grain bin and the gate, park the Jeep. Then with the tire tool, I break the padlock and the chain off the garage door. It is a machine shop as I suspected. I find a hammer and wire cutter. I cut two one foot lengths of wire from the fence and wire the chain across the opening of the grain bin. Hopefully that will slow them. Then I cut the top strand of barbed wire free from the fence post closest to the grain bin. I go to the next post and cut the wire there. I swing the free end of the wire back across the pasture side of the grain bin and wire it down to the post on that side. If anyone hits this they will be in for a jolt.

Now I feel safer. I break out the back window of the Jeep. I will feel like a fool if they don't come now. I line up the boxes of shells I have left against the rear wall of the Jeep. Then I fill the two glass gallon jugs with gas and put their caps back on. I put the five gallon gas container in the back also with whatever gas is left. I put one on the gallons of gas on the floor in the middle of the grain bin. I grab some paper, corn cobs, and sticks and build a small fire. It should burn for at least fifteen minutes.

I drive the Jeep about twenty-five feet into the pasture area. Then I take out the Nagant, lay it across the hood of the Jeep. Click off the safety and wait. I take off my shoes leaving my socks on. Take off my shirt and rub my body with dirt. I light another cigar. Perhaps my last. Surprisingly calm, I wait. My time estimate turns out to be fairly accurate. I had to wait less than three minutes after completing my welcoming chores before the first bike turned onto the farm entrance.

Once three bikes have turned onto the driveway, I begin firing the Nagant. When it is empty, I throw it into the Jeep and pull out the Benelli. By now they are at the grain bin chain. I fire at the bottle and break it. The gas ignites and several bikers run screaming from the bin. I see several bikes now going back down the driveway. They are attempting to flank me. I fire at the bikers until the magazine is empty. Rounds are being fired at me also, but I stand mostly behind the Jeep. Now I jump in and drive as rapidly as I can for the corner of the pasture. It's hard to tell if I hurt any of them but I saw at least three bikes go down. There is an explosion that lights up the sky. I am over the hill by now, trying not to break an axle or get stuck. That would mean death. None the less, I need to beat the cycles that are coming down the road toward the broken fence.

My left forearm is very painful. I can feel blood pouring out. Damn. I tear off a strip of duct tape, wrap it around the wound as tightly as I can while steering with my injured arm. I see the fence is still down, I go through and up on the river road and roar north as fast as the Jeep can take me.   I manage to get there two good blocks before the bikers.

I try to reload the Benelli now but my left hand is not working too well.   I steer with left hand and point the Remington over the rear seat. I can see the lights in my rear view mirror now but they are still at a good distance. Closing rapidly. Damned motorcycles are fast.   By the time I cross the bridge some are within twenty yards of me. I fire off the Remington, then bank into a hard right turn sailing off the road and onto the parking lot of the abandoned Aragorn ballroom. I straighten the Jeep out, speed up and drive toward the broken dam forty yards down. I break the glass bottle with the Remington barrel, jump from the Jeep, strike one of the kitchen matches, toss it in back, and run for the river.

I dive out as far as I can, I know right below the burst dam here is the deepest part of the Jim River. I can hear them shooting at me and the fired rounds going ffisshingg past until I am under water. I am still underwater when the concussion hits me. An explosion rocks me just as I am struck on my right buttock. The force twists me about underwater. Not a great amount of pain, not like what I would have expected.   The explosion of the Jeep was incredible and almost knocked me out under water. When I surface I see several people on fire and running, back by the burning Jeep. I see more bikers watching the river, and I see two men swimming in the river. Rounds immediately begin to land near me in the river and I submerge again. I let the current carry me downstream toward the Missouri. My strength is ebbing and I am unable to swim as well as I usually can. I draw my knife and close on the first swimmer. He is battling to keep his head out of the water. I suspect he didn't know we were going swimming and forgot to take off his boots, chains or colors before coming in after me. I approach him head on and when he attempts to grab me, I slice his left arm with the knife. He clutches his arm with his right hand, swinging slightly to the right. He is trying to evade me now, but I thrust with my arms and legs, come about two feet out of the water and as I come down I drive the K-BAR deep into his throat. Damn, I cannot pull it out as he sinks. The other biker has seen what I did and is wary. Still, he is moose-like in the water, dog paddling, barely staying afloat. I stay out of his reach for minutes while he tires, then submerge, come up behind him. I lunge onto his back and lock both arms around his head. His head is forced underwater by the additional weight. He thrashes around violently and almost throws me off. His actions grow less, and soon I feel no movements at all. I continue to ride him, holding his head under for at least ten minutes while we continue floating toward the big river.

Where the two rivers merge, I release him and swim to the shore on the side near Memorial Park.

The shore is a steep rocky bank ten feet high, covered with rocks, grass and loose dirt. It is difficult to climb because I am totally spent. I flop down to rest when I reach level ground. Wet jeans, tee shirt and socks. I am very cold in the nighttime breeze. I stand finally. The night is silent. No unnatural sounds. I can hear the wind blowing against the trees, fish splashing in the Missouri, even the cars moving in town and driving over the bridge there on Highway 81. I can hear nobody near me now. The park is deserted, not unusual for this early in the morning. I find it difficult to walk. My right leg causes severe pain near my hip. I struggle to get to my rental car but find the keys have been removed from under the rock. Someone is here. I have been betrayed. It's not possible that the key was accidentally found. Fight or Flight? Has to be flight. I am exhausted, have no weapons. I walk down the fence row east back to the confluence of the Jim and Missouri rivers. Whoever is coming will be coming from the main entrance area to the park. I hear no boat engines, so I discount the possibility that a boat is coming. I walk to the far eastern corner of the fence surrounding the water plant. Looking north I see the

Jeep still burning two blocks up the river on the opposite side. I find a walk space between the river's edge and the fence. It will be tight and overgrown with weeds and scrub trees, but I believe I can do it. I stop there. Waiting, watching to the west.

I see a man walking slowly toward the car. He is cautious. looking slowly around as he walks. I don't see any weapons but I could easily miss them in the dark. It is who I expected. It's the bartender.

"Stop there," I say loudly. "If you leave now you won't have to die."

He continues to slowly walk at me.

I can wait no longer. I turn north and squeeze between the fence and a small tree. Growth pulls at my feet, I force myself forward. I have gone at least ten yards into the overgrowth when I hear him shoot at me. I hear the round zip past. A very unpleasant sound. I pull myself forward faster. If he can get close enough or get lucky enough, I'm toast. Two more explosions behind me and two more rounds whistle through the trees around me.

I bend down and grab the base of a small scrub tree. Swing my feet over the edge of the river bank slowly. The bank here falls almost straight down to the river, a drop of about seven feet. I let myself down as far as I can, gripping the edge of the bank, then let go and fall several feet into the soft mud of the river. I lean into the bank, smear mud on my face, and stand as motionless as possible. I can hear him moving in the brush above me. I hear him shoot again. No sound of a bullet going past. Good, he doesn't know where I am. I stand and wait. Soon I can no longer hear him. I wait. Ten or twenty minutes I wait, hard to tell time in the cold. I know he could be standing waiting also but I have to move. Hypothermia is also waiting to get me, this thick coating of mud is not keeping me very warm.

I move into the river silently, dog paddling and letting the current take me along. When I reach the confluence, I pull myself up where the shore is the shallowest. Easier to climb up here. Once out, I lay quietly assessing the pain and my abilities to move. This additional chase has pulled much of my will power out and let it float away with the river. I hold my butt with my right hand attempting to staunch the flow. I try to pull myself up on the rocky rip-rap dumped there to prevent the Missouri from washing the land away when the Jim river floods. I lay quietly, cannot hear anyone else in the park. I am astonished at the amount of pain produced by two little bullet holes. Apparently the cold, mud, and time since being shot have all contributed to more pain for Matt. My forearm is on fire and my butt is screaming at me 'don't move.' I know I must move or I will die here. The cold will do me in before too long. My body says, 'just rest one more minute.' If I can get to the top of the bank, the ground will be level and the cold water from the rivers will no longer blow onto me. Maybe I can dry off a bit. I wiggle my way to one of the larger rocks and grasp it with both hands, trying to lift myself off the ground. I struggle to get my feet under me and begin to stand ignoring the waves of pain moving through me. I stop half-way up to wait out the dizziness. If I pass out here I will be turtle food. Finally I can stand erect.

I am shivering violently from the cold but I do take that first step. I move my left leg ten inches. Way to go Matt. I lean on to the left leg and then drag my right leg forward. I look at the top of the bank, roughly calculating, I need another twelve steps to get to level ground. Easy as sucking clotted cream. I thrust my left leg out again, maybe even twelve inches this time, lean into it and drag my right leg up even. Perhaps I should sit and rest a minute on this rock. No..No..No.. Take another step. Lean into it, drag right leg up. Almost there now. I find the pain to be a constant now. It is so unbearable that I can't ignore it. One more thrust forward with the left leg, lean into it and disaster, my foot slips on the wet ground and down I tumble. I have been able to twist my body so I land on my right leg making the pain grow desperate for my attention. I move my body into crawling formation and begin pulling myself up with my hands and arms. A pull with my arms, a push with my left leg, repeat. I continue moving, refusing to stop. If I stop, I will slide backward into a wet eternity. And just like that, I make it. My arms and upper body are on level ground. I decide to watch quietly to see if anyone is around. If the guy is here. I am dead. I will never escape him again.

I rest, my hand squeezing to stop the bleeding of my buttock. I can feel warmth with my hand so I believe I am losing some blood. Slowly now I open my eyes. I could have slept some, but it is still dark. I need to move. Something about cold and wet is dangerous but I can't remember now what it is. I try to stand. I push up with both hands, lifting my butt into the air and walking backward with my hands until I can get my balance and stand half way up. Stop there and wait for the dizziness to pass. I wobble, I stand erect, I have done it. I am Superman. I can see the bridge now. It has lights along the upper rail. I see no one lurking around to kill me or help me. I take a step. Left leg out, ten inches, lean into it, drag right leg forward. I am still on the dirt road, one block ahead is the asphalt road, and two blocks further is the bridge. Take a step, lean into it, drag right leg. Already I have come twenty inches. I'm not going to die here. I can make it, I can live.

I know that if certain people are out here looking for me they will hurt me more, but I cannot remember why. How many steps are in one block, I think one hundred yards is about a block, there are about four of my steps in each yard, so if I just step four hundred or six hundred more times I can rest and will be okay. Thrust with left leg, lean into it and drag your right leg, it's a snap. No pain..No pain..No pain.. Thrust with left leg, lean into it and drag your other leg. Almost there now, Drill Sergeant, almost there.

The man who followed me past the water treatment plant was not a biker. I remember that. He was connected to them some way but I didn't know how. Alisha is connected to the bikers, also. She tried to kill me, I know she is bad. Somehow I will work this out, the two of them are the evil and I need to figure it out. There is the other bartender, also. He is a gang informer. I take a step, lean into it, drag leg. Why did they want to kill me? There was something about fires and shooting. Why does he want to rob me? It's there at the edge of my consciousness. Whatever I did, I'm sorry. There is still a wind blowing, but my clothes have dried and I am not so tired now. I bump into something big. The bridge. I made it to the bridge. I walk under the bridge on to a dry area, cocoon myself as best I can with gathered leaves and grass and I lay down. I am better as the wall of the dam keeps the wind from swirling around me. I have to get warm. I snuggle as deeply into the dust and bridge wall as I can. Soon blackness comes.

The rest of the night comes and goes in blurs as I wake with starts, then fall slowly back to sleep. Mostly cups of steaming coffee and large plates of spaghetti with huge meatballs filled what dreams I can recall. I frequently see Alisha and the two bartenders coming near and calling my name. I never answer them. My skin feels like it is burned. I see the sky starting to lighten. Then I find myself fully awake with the sound of traffic moving over me on the bridge. It is full daylight now.

I begin the torture of movement. I need to stand. First, I roll onto my stomach which I can actually do. Push that butt into the air with hands and knees. I begin walking backward with my hands. Feet are braced solid so my body actually begins to rise. I move into areas of too much pain and drop back down to sitting. I wiggle my feet and hands. Get the circulation moving, when I warm up it will be easier. I cannot stop myself from shivering violently, my whole lower jaw is chattering with the cold. Fuck! Fuck! Fuck! I need to get warm. I cover myself and sit still.

CHAPTER TWENTY-NINE

I hear a car stop near me on the gravel, maybe fifteen yards away. I stay as silent as I can.

"Matt?" Matt?" Are you down here?"

"Uuugghyah." I finally grunt out. "Here...Over here." I can't see who it is but I have lost my fear of capture with the specter of death sitting on my shoulder.

The Sheriff is standing above me now. "Let's get you in the car." He grabs my hand and pulls me to my feet. Easy when you are warm. I close my eyes.

"It's only pain."

"Can you walk?" Thatcher asks me.

"Slowly, I got shot in the ass and arm. And I am cold. I think I can walk." Left leg forward, then drag right leg, repeat. Incredibly, as I walk further the pain recedes and I can walk faster.

The Sheriff opens the back door to the car, "In here. And lay down." He shuts the door, gets in front, turns the heat on high, and drives. God, the heat feels wonderful. I start to shake violently.

I suppose in a way I am lucky to be so cold. I am not worried about jail, imminent incarceration followed by a painful death. Also, I have not lost as much blood as I would have if I had been warm.

The car stops. "I'm at the convenience store. Keep your head down. I'll be right back. Damn it, Matt, keep your head down. We're both screwed if someone sees you now."

He gets back in, drives ten minutes and stops. "Okay, sit up." I keep lying down. "Go ahead, you can sit up here." Nothing from me but moans.

He gets out, opens the rear door, grabs my shoulder and sets me up. "Here this will help." He puts one of those Mexican blankets on me, wraps it around my feet and stretches it up to tuck under my chin. "Take this." He hands me a cup of steaming coffee. "Take these." He has four capsules in his hand, "Antibiotics. Your wounds are full of mud. These should help stave off the infection."

"Thanks, I'm sure I need them. Coffee is wonderful." He also hands me a white bag with several donuts in it. I stuff them in my mouth, I am so hungry. My face and hands are so dirty I am eating as much dirt as donut and do not care. Can't remember my last meal. Certainly it didn't taste as good as this. I am beginning to beat the cold. My shivering is now decreasing. It's no longer ferocious, just violent.

"No jokes about cops and donuts. It's all they had in there." The Sheriff looks back at me and smiles. Nice smile. He looks to be in late fifties, friendly face, above average tall, little over weight, and he has one of the knob knocker ugly hats these western acting doodahs wear.

"You saved my life with donuts and hot coffee, Sheriff. Thanks for getting me."

"Sorry I didn't get you sooner. I figured out where you were around four in the morning. Truth of it is you made such a mess of those "Sabata" ding dongs that I couldn't get away. From the time you shot the guy up in Lester, until we got the last guy to the hospital or morgue, I was running. I left Frank and my other deputy, Anders, to finish the clean-up. Just between you and me, I don't think that gang wants to see all that much of you, anymore.

"Am I under arrest?"

"Matt, look around, does it look like I am going toward the jail or am I going out of town? Has your brain quit working? And call me John, okay? Anyway, you are just a homeless guy I found in Memorial Park after a biker gang battle. You were hit by several stray bullets and almost died of hypothermia. Now I am taking you somewhere to get you healed up. If I take you to the hospital, the gang will hear about it and toast your bagel. If I take you to a Doctor, he has to report all gunshot wounds, then put you in the hospital. Again you are toast. It's the law. I am taking you to a lady from the Arikara Sioux Indian tribe who is known for her ability to heal. She doesn't have to report to anyone but her husband. Truth be told, I think he answers to her: she is one tough lady."

The landscape is changing as we ride. Soon after leaving Tanley, the land flattens out. The hills and valleys forced on the land by the Jim and Missouri rivers irons out to a gently rolling terrain. The drive was at least a half an hour. I assume we are traveling north and west. I believe the town we went through last was Wagoner. Sheriff John slows and turns into a long driveway.

"You will like this couple, both are the genuine article."

The homestead seems familiar with the large red barn and the tall squarish white house dominating everything. There is a wide wind break of cedar and Russian olive trees to the left and rear of the house. Attached to the barn and running the full length of one side is a large fenced in and screened area. Chickens are squawking and flapping at our approach. The house has a full unscreened porch running the full length of both sides that I can see. There is a pack of five or six dogs yapping and barking at us. I see five smaller buildings scattered about the lot and under the huge cottonwood tree that dominates the front yard is an older well used pickup truck.

A tall man and short woman wait near the walkway leading to the house. John pulls up next to them. And begins to open his door. "Howdy, Anne and Bruce. This is the guy I called you about."

Anne goes over to John and the two begin talking. I push my door open and attempt to swing my feet out of the car. Nothing is cooperating. My legs catch on the hump and the door well; I try to force them through the obstacles but have little strength. The injuries and the cold have combined to limit my movement. I am warm now but my body remembers. Pain has come back with a new level slightly above intolerable. Thatcher is standing by the open door reaching in to help me stand.

A mountain moves past him, nudges him out of the way and with an easy movement, sweeps me up in his arms and carries me down the path to his house, up the stairs to the porch where he opens the front door, and effortlessly carries me up the stairs to the second floor. There he deposits me in the bathtub. I weigh two hundred and twenty pounds; I'm stunned at this man's incredible strength. He is at least three inches taller than me and fifty pounds heavier, with long black hair tied behind his back. He has remained silent.

"Thanks," I mumble. He takes out a cigarette, lights it, and offers it to me. I take a big drag and inhale deeply. Like I say, when the whole world falls in on you and you're ass deep in alligators, a smoke helps. He holds my cigarette while Anne uses scissors to cut up the back of my shirt, then my jeans and underwear. She holds a bowl of warm water that she uses to soak the clothing from front to back. It's warm and doesn't hurt. However, she starts to tug at the shirt which is well attached to my skin with dried blood and dirt. Tug, tug, dab, dab. While she is working on the shirt, I push down on my jeans and work at getting my underwear free. The blood has clotted and dried at several sensitive places and I believe I am best qualified to handle this part. I am past modesty but too many, really sensitive, things can get caught when removing underwear. Once I am shirt, underwear, and jeans free, she gently lifts each foot and removes the socks.

The scrub begins, which I will always remember as the most pain ever inflicted on a human being with the purpose of trying to help them. First the water starts, a nice temperature, flows over my head and down my body. Actually feels good. John and Anne pour on shampoo and begin to scrub my head, then the rest of me with what feels like wire brushes but I suspect are actually washcloths to spread soap over my body. I notice that the water in the bottom of the tub makes a colorful display of browns and reds. The bigger clots look strange in a bathtub, they collect at the drain, blocking some of the water. As they scrub the rest of me, I am hoping John is doing the male parts. Bruce hands my smoke back to me. He motions for me to inhale and hold it. The man has given me a joint, not a cigarette. I drag deeply and hold. I cough with the harshness of the smoke. Not a wise thing to do. Pain is there to be paid for such actions. Then I feel like some of the pain is actually subsiding. Incredible. While there are two people inflicting pain, he is helping. Again he motions. I take another huge toke. Then he takes it from me as they dry me down. Bruce lifts me out of the tub and sets me down next to it.

I am able to walk into the bedroom. White sheets cover the whole bed. I lay on my stomach with the pillows under my chest. Anne's face wrinkles in concentration as she begins to work on my forearm. She says something curt to Bruce. He leaves, returning immediately with a large floor lamp which she positions over my arm. She cuts off the duct tape, then shaves my forearm on both sides around the wound, I turn my head so I can't watch.

Bruce is watching. He hands me a pint bottle and motions for me to take a drink. I believe him and drink deeply. Whiskey, cheap whiskey. He hands me the joint again. I am watching him and ignoring the fact that his wife has poured kerosene on my arm and is now lighting it on fire. I suspect soon there will be little left below the elbow. I can't move it because John has a grip on it and he's stronger than me from this angle. Bruce hands me the bottle again. I like cheap whiskey. Anne is using a pick and shovel to work on my arm. I am certain that she has climbed up on the bed and is stomping the dressing deep in the wound hole with her foot. When I look, I see that she has covered the wound with a poultice and white gauze and is now wrapping both sides with an ace bandage. 'Ah ha, the hard part is over' thinks I. I hear tape tear and just like that she is finished with my arm.

I am grateful. I can use some sleep. Bruce nudges me again. He hands me the bottle. I drink, I finish the bottle and hand it back. He hands me the joint, I inhale deeply and hold it. She sticks the forceps into the wound on my butt and I straighten out like a kite string in a hurricane. My God, that hurts. I can feel her pull the side of the wound apart, stretching the actual size of the tear. At first she's holding it open with her fingers, then she begins using her hands. Pulling it apart with one hand on each side. She is looking into the wound by moving her head from side to side. "Here look at this," she says to John. Then she stretches the opening another six inches or so and she sticks her whole head in to look around. "Can you see what I'm looking at here?" Obviously this is not sufficient so she stretches the opening another six or eight inches and gets most of one arm in also. Now she is holding it open with a foot on one side and a hand on the other. John hasn't answered fast enough, so the next thing I know she pulls his head inside also. Fuck- fuck- fuck ...I am worried that she is going to invite Bruce in for a look also when I hear her say. "Here it is."

She shows me the bullet. The pain rapidly subsides and I put my head down. She is putting a bandage over the wound. "Take these." She sticks two pills in my mouth and gives me a little water to drink. Time to sleep.

I don't remember the rest of the day. I wake the next day bandaged, lame, stiff and sore, and needing to pee. I try to sit. Ouch! My head hurts. My butt hurts. Surprisingly my arm is not really too bad.

Pain has decided that I should not just sit up. I stay on my stomach and slide one leg over the edge. Once I feel the floor, I swing my body so that both legs are off the bed with my feet on the floor. I begin pushing myself off the bed and onto my feet. I stand, at last, with my hands still on the bed for balance but my weight is on my feet. Wait for the nausea and dizziness to subside and then I let go of the bed and stand free. It is painful but I am the one doing it. Hey, hey, it's independence. I take one step toward the door. Ouch! I step with my left leg, then drag my right leg up even. Then step again with the left leg, lean into it, drag right leg even. I will make it to the bedroom door. Hooray! I can see the bathroom. I try to lead with my right leg but can only take a tiny step. Follow with the left, then the right; I am walking. I make it to the toilet. A major battle has been fought here in South Dakota, land of the battling brave, and won on the field of pain and bathroom privileges.

I turn and see Anne looking at me. She is so cute standing there looking at me with what I think is a look of disapproval. I expect she will be angry that I am out of bed. Or maybe, she will be impressed that I battled my way to the bathroom. Nah, not this warrior woman from the plains. She circles me and examines my bandages. Doesn't look too worried. Pokes me here and there. She turns from me, "Bruce," she calls. He is beside me in less than two minutes. I think he will take me to bed. However, Anne says, "Help him balance when he walks downstairs."

He lightly takes my right elbow. I say to him "She is tough to please." We walk to the steps and take the first one down, using my left leg in front, bending my right knee. It is more agony than I think I can bear. I turn to return to bed but Bruce does not release my elbow. He pulls and I have to take the next step down. "You are not all that easy either, are you?" I say. I think this much pain could be a fatal amount, but I can't turn back. By the third step I begin to feel the pain is lessening. Not enough that I want to continue, but again I have no choice and I have to finish these stairs.

Anne walks past us saying, "I'll set the table for breakfast." Bruce keeps dragging me down the stairs. I actually feel like I am descending from the Washington Monument. Finally we make it, get to the table and sit. Surprisingly, it's the bending to sit that is painful, not the actual sitting. And it has all been worth it because Anne has bacon and eggs for breakfast. She puts a good half pound of crisp bacon on my plate with two eggs over easy and there is a plate of toast to share. This lady is a cook. She brings me a glass of water and gives me two capsules of what I believe are antibiotic. Plus coffee, don't let me forget the coffee, hot and thick. Strong as Wild West coffee should be. This is the kind of coffee they gave Wyatt Earp before they told him to take care of that little fracas down at the Okay Corral.

Bruce went "Mm mm."

I am sitting on the porch with Bruce two days later. Dogs are running everywhere. Noise, at least farm noise is a constant out here. No radio or television that I have seen so far. Anne has turned out to be a wonderful medicine woman. She has Bruce as her physical therapist. Once he grabs your arm, you will walk where he wants to walk. He has remained silent, but he seems to be a nice man. I have come to enjoy the mornings sitting on the porch. My wounds are left open now for the air to heal, according to Anne.

When I inquire, she tells me her actual name was Catchesbee Makes-room. But it was changed to Anne Gaddy at reservation school. Bruce's Sioux Indian name is Bear Coup Makes-room-for-plenty. He goes by Bruce Ramsey. They are the people of the Lakota Sioux Tribe. The specific tribe they had belonged to and still belong to and will always belong to is the Arikara Sioux. Their great chief was Plenty Coup perhaps the greatest of all Sioux warriors. She said Bruce had wandered away from his home when he was young and all thought he had been lost, but they found him on the prairie playing with a black bear cub. That was how he received his name, he had counted coup on a baby bear!

Bruce nudges me and stands up. I know this meant that I should accompany him. We walk out into his yard through the gate and across the road into the wild prairie grass. We walk another two blocks, with pain in my stride still there, I am not enthusiastic at walking yet. Then Bruce stops and looks at me. He points north, then south. It is a question. I pick south. We walk a block south and then turn and begin walking back to the house. We walk directly into a patch of small cacti. Bruce cuts one of them out by the roots, puts it in his leather pouch and we walk back to the porch.

Anne brings us out a glass of lemonade and two small empty plates. She wants to know how I am feeling and warns me to not let Bruce wear me out. She says I will be able to leave in another day or two. I am healing nicely and there is nothing more she can do to help me. Bruce takes out the cactus, trims the thorns and offers a piece to Anne first. She declines with a slight wave of her hand. He offers it to me. He eats a piece himself. What could I do but eat the piece?

He says, "Good."

"Bruce, you talk." I say, astonished.

"You must not have said anything too stupid. Apparently he likes you. He has shown you how to find the proper peyote for you," Says Anne.

He puts two small pieces of the cactus on the plate and hands the plate to me. Then trims up another couple of pieces for himself. We watch the dogs and the beautiful cloud formations in the sky. I am a little startled when a large white owl comes and sits on the railing of the porch. It stares at me. I think it is easily the most beautiful owl ever.

I am puzzled by the owl, clearly it wants me to do something but I just can't understand.

Bruce nudges me again. We stand and go down from the porch. The owl goes before us. Maybe it is leading Bruce. It flies into a small garage type shed. Bruce follows the owl inside. I see the body of a biker, draped over the bike. The owl who is sitting above us in the rafters says, "He came last night. He made a mistake when he threatened Anne."

Bruce looks at the owl for a while. Then he looks at me. "Let's bury this white piece of trash." He hands me a shovel. I start to dig. He stops me immediately. "Do you not see that the grave should be dug over there." He points to a patch of ground outside the garage and I can see it. It is so obvious, the energy swirls in gray lines around one patch of ground. The dirt within appears lifeless. I start digging there. It goes very fast as some sort of energy seems to have removed much of the weight of the dirt. Also, Bruce knows how to use a shovel. I try to help, but he ends up doing ninety percent of the digging. He digs a huge deep hole. He is a force of nature. I would like to see him swing a golf club some time. The owl says, "Never happen."

The biker goes into the grave first, then the bike. I never find out how Bruce killed him but I like to think that Coup Bear gave him a bear hug and just crushed him to death. I am very fond of Bruce and like to think of him as a brother.

I doubt he would ever admit to having emotions even if he has them.

Sheriff John visits on my third day with the Ramseys. By now I am managing the stairs by myself and I will spend some time everyday just walking around the yard and looking at the garden. I usually spend some time throwing stuff for the dogs. Anne and Bruce have been absent for a while, but their pickup is parked under the cottonwood so they are here someplace.

"You're looking to be feeling somewhat better, Matt."

"Oh yeah. Life looks more like it's here to stay, today. That night under the bridge was close. I could have died there and not felt any worse. But now I am ready. I am getting back to my fighting weight with all the good stuff here."

"I'm figuring another day or two and then it's time to leave. What are you thinking? I haven't talked to Anne yet, but you are looking pretty spry."

"What do I pay them, John? I owe them so much. Crap, I am even wearing their clothes. I thought about going to Parkston to get some money but they would want some identification before they would give me any money. Everything I had was lost in the fire. Can you get my stuff like a Driver's license or my passport for me?"

"We can work on that back in Tanley. I did get a bag of clothes for you at Goodwill." He goes to his car and comes back with a big plastic bag. "I guessed at the size. You never were that spiffy, anyway."

"Taking care of the Ramseys is my business, too, because I brought you here and they did it as a favor to me. Paying them is tough. I know they wouldn't take money. That would be an insult, so I bought them a young buffalo. It's being processed now and will be delivered tomorrow when I come up to get you. Now, here's the thing, don't tell them. Certainly don't suggest that it's payment. When I come I will tell them I brought something for their next family get-together. Their family will consume the whole beast, but it will give them an immense amount of pride to provide the meat."

We sit for a minute and just look out at the yard and across the road to the prairie. This is truly beautiful country. "John, I tell you the truth. I envy these two. They live in paradise. They have all they need and they are devoted to each other. It feels to me like God lives close to here."

"Are you thinking of moving up here?"

"Can't, you know I would be the serpent. Too many bad guys always watching for me. It would ruin paradise for them."

"Do you want to know how you did that night in Tanley?" John asks.

"Been wondering about that. Do you suppose they remember me at CHICKS?"

"They remember, trust me. They are hoping you're dead and floating down the Missouri. Right now, I am counting only eight members still hanging around and three of them are limping. Brode is there and healthy. Four members are still in the hospital. You have worked miracles on improving the economy of the Harley-Davidson factory in Milwaukee and there is a flower shop in Yankton that thinks you are a semi-god. The bad news is CHICKS BAR is still going. They have reopened the strip bars in Lester and Avalon. Motels are in action again, also. The members have to work hard to keep everything protected. Still, they are forming up and will be strong again."

"Well, John, just so you know my version, they were attacking me, I was only defending myself. What I did, I did just to survive."

"Oh bite me in the ass with that bull shit. You set them up, provoked them, then led them into your trap. You outfoxed them the whole way. All I can say is 'bravo,' way to go. If we had ten more men like you in the county, they wouldn't have ever got a toe hold in."

"Well, maybe I did provoke them a touch."

"When you come back to Tanley, do you want to be my deputy? You know they can't touch you when you put the badge on."

"Damn John, you got a wicked sense of humor. That would be funny," I say.

"I am serious, Matt. With you as my deputy, we can clean the county up."

"Thanks for the offer, John, but If you sign me on as a deputy you would have the mayor and the city council on your neck. Also, I know that somewhere in the oath of office I would have to swear to uphold the laws. I take my vows seriously and I believe I will have to kill a couple more people before this is through. The person who killed Jennie is still walking. I am going to kill that person."

"You know who killed her don't you? I was watching your face and it dawned on me, you know her killer."

"Yep, I know."

"And you are not going to tell me?"

"No way in hell do I tell you."

"Why not?" asks John.

"Because you are the Sheriff. You would have to do Sheriffy shit. You would arrest he-she-them and charge them with murder. Then they would go to trial and be acquitted. And presto, they would disappear into the ether.

Never to be seen again. That's the long answer, John. The short answer is the legal system would fuck it up."

"You sound like you don't think much of me."

"Quite the opposite, John. I think you are Jake, strait up, a genuine tall man. But you work in a corrupt country against both bad guys and unknown forces. They work together to stop you at every turn. Look at your Deputy Frank, another genuine nice guy. He is so wrapped up in all that legal hogwash-guilt-indecision, and fear of not doing the right thing that he has a hard time getting dressed in the morning. Christ, John, he knew who had murdered his son for two years and did nothing but plan."

"Well, let me get your take on my plans, okay?"

"Sure"

"I found finger prints on an empty ammonia bottle and traced the location of the guy to a rented farm house. I think he is the source of most of the meth. The still is located just north east of town about two miles. I plan on hitting it and destroying the cooker soon. That will start to cut into the money production of the gang. If you would like to come along, we can hit it tomorrow night."

"Hell yes, I am with you," I say.

"Investigating Jennie's death, I have found a witness who tells me that Alisha visited Jennie that morning. Right now the witness won't testify. If I can find supporting evidence, maybe I can bring her to trial. I know you had visited her socially for a while so I thought I better tell you."

"We are totally split. No worries."

"Thirdly, I am having my late night deputy, Anders drive through Avalon and Lester every night. I have him spend at least a half an hour in each town. Park in front of the motels, take pictures of guys going in the bars. That type of thing. If we can discourage some of their customers, maybe we can hurt them more."

"Damn John, you have the reins in your teeth and are True Gritting your way right into these bastards. Glad I will be there to help."

"Coming back to get you tomorrow afternoon if Anne lets me."

"Okay, big man, I'll be ready."

CHAPTER THIRTY

The funeral director called all of Jennie's family into the chapel for an intimate prayer before services. She looked cold and waxy in the coffin. Everyone said how natural she looked.

In the church he spoke the necessary platitudes. "We are gathered here in the presence of God to say farewell to our beloved Jennie Johnson." There were a few hymns, a few sniffles, a few more platitudes to allay everyone's fear of death. Then, "Would you like to say a few words, Frank?"

He looked at the families, his and hers. Sitting on different sides of the church. Everyone seemed locked into their own stupid tradition.

"She was my all, what I got up for, what I went to work for, what I lived for, and probably what I will die for. Now, she has died. My former life has to die, also."

"Ecclesiastes 7: 8, says "Better is the end of a thing than its beginning."

"As my new life begins, I say this is the beginning of the end to those who caused my Jennie to come to this place. I should have been at the side of my friend. Instead, I was on the side of the law. That ends now."

He left the church with that and returned to his house. No more funeral tradition for him. She would be buried while he is starting to plan his future.

CHAPTER THIRTY-ONE

John is swearing me in as a special deputy. He picked me up at Anne and Bruce's this morning and we are going to hit the meth cooker today if he can get the search warrant. I have a badge now but only for today. I make a sandwich while he goes to see the Judge. Deputies Johnson, Anders, and Smith are all here at the table eating, too. Sheriff Thatcher comes in, says, "I got it. Let's roll" and we are off. I am riding with Frank. I am thinking that first part of the raid where we drive into the farm will be the most dangerous.

"Do you have any of the pistols left?" I ask Frank. "All of my firearms were destroyed when the Jeep burned."

"I still have the Ruger revolver if you want it." I take it. "Remember," he says, "It only holds five rounds and it's going to kick, big time. It is a three fifty seven."

"I'll remember," I promise him.

Nothing exciting happens. The man does not resist, we find the cooker and destroy it, taking pictures for evidence. Frank puts the man in handcuffs. We search for a while but there is nothing out here but a filthy house. We head back to town. I turn my badge back in to John. We finish our lunch. The man is already bailed out. Still, it will take time to replace the hardware and the gang's money will be impacted.

CHAPTER THIRTY-TWO

I leave John's house early in the morning, about three o'clock. I go out the back of John's, walk slowly toward the alley behind Alisha's house. I am wearing dark clothes and a cap. I see no one else out walking and only one car several blocks off.

I come up behind her garage and try the door. Still open. I go in and quietly close the door. I have been curious about what she is doing. None of the deputies have seen her for the last week. Her car is not in the garage. That is suspicious. She may well be gone. It's possible that she has loaned out her car, but that's unlikely. I set up one of her lawn chairs and sit watching her house through the window in the front of her garage. Time for a little illegal surveillance.

I had been sitting for thirty minutes and was just pulling out a cigar when I saw movement in her kitchen window. 'Yes, she is here. Just avoiding people.' I take out the Ruger and lay it in my lap, just in case. It gradually becomes light out. I still am unsure of who I have seen in the window. Could use some binoculars.

I assume by now that Alisha would be up making tea. Her kitchen lights should be on. The house is dark. I see the side door open and a small figure in dark clothes and a green cap walks back toward the garage. I can hear him pass quickly along the side. Then silence, I listen, sit quietly for at least ten minutes. Nothing is moving. I walk out, look around but can see no one. I go back into the garage and put the chair away.

Let's see if that girl is in there. I go to her door and as quietly as I can, I walk in. Stop. Listen. This is an empty house. The sound of someone in the house is always there. It may be subtle but it's there. There is no one here. I go to her bedroom and put on the light. The green cap man has been staying here.

Alisha has gone. I still have a burn to get revenge for Jennie. I will find Alisha.

I go back to the living room. Sit in the big chair, put my gun in my lap and my knife on the arm of the chair. This guy didn't believe me back in Nebraska. Time to convince him. I call Frank and then John to warn them that green cap is out there and may be watching them. While I wait, I think about where Alisha has gone. I know she has not gone far enough.

It is late afternoon when I hear the side door open. I pick up the Ruger and hold it before me, aiming it at the door leading from the kitchen to the living room. I hear the faucet come on and then shut off. I hear the refrigerator door open and then shut. He comes through the door with a bottle of water in his hand. Stops when he sees me with the gun aimed at him.

"Good afternoon, Green Cap Hitman," I say. "I was hoping you took my advice and went home."

"Sorry," he says, "I just couldn't leave without seeing you again."

"Here I am. Have you seen enough of me yet?"

"If you let me, I will leave right now."

"First you need to tell me if you killed the woman or Alisha did?" I ask.

"She did."

I pull the trigger hitting him in the middle of his chest. The kick almost breaks my arm but it picks him up off the floor several inches and throws him back against the kitchen cabinets. He crumples to the floor like a broken doll. The roar in an enclosed room is incredible. I can hear nothing but buzzing in my ears. I know I have to leave quick, someone must have heard and called that in.

Poor old Green Hat. He thought I really wanted to know if he killed her. Being there and not stopping it was death sentence enough for me.

I pick up my stuff, wipe down the coffee table where I sat and go to the side door. The guy is still alive. He kicks me in the back on my right knee, smashes me into the door and almost knocks me down. I whirl with my knife in my right hand ready for him. He is up now and reaching into his vest to get his pistol. I run at him and he tries to fend me off with his knee, which hits my thigh, and his arm which I brush aside as my own right arm descends with my knife. I drive my knife downward into his chest from its entry point in his throat. He goes over backward as I keep running and pushing at him. I fall on top of him and hold the arm which is going for his pistol. I just lay still and look in his eyes. He knows he is dying and has ceased to struggle. Our eyes are inches apart. For the first time in my life, I see life leave another person's eyes. One moment there is life, then nothing but an empty shell.

I pull my knife out, wash it in the sink. I take his billfold and his pistol, pick up the stuff I dropped when he kicked me. I leave out the side door and walk back past the garage into the alley and then down to the street.

Frank pulls up next to me. Cuffs me and puts me in the back seat. "You are under arrest. You have the right," he keeps on mumbling such crap as he heads back to drive. We go to John's house, pull into the garage. He takes off the cuffs and helps me out. "Damn you make a lot of noise."

We go into John's kitchen. He is already at the table with coffee and he waves us to help ourselves. I tell them what happened and that the hit man is dead.

"Here is his stuff." I put his pistol and billfold on the table.

John picks it up, shoves the money at me, "I am going to run this and see what I can find out about him. Let's just leave him lay in case Alisha come home. Sort of a present to her."

Frank pushes something at me too. It's my passport. "I couldn't get your driver's license. Too much red tape there in Florida. Why don't you just get one here?"

"Sure, that's good for me."

"Okay, I will have Rosa run it tomorrow. She will do it so much faster than me. I swear those poges at state are terrified of her.

"I'm off on patrol. First the bar, then Lester, then Avalon, then something for supper. What do you think, meet here at seven?"

"Hell, yes," we say in chorus.

John adds, "Either Chinese or pizza. I'm happy with either. I am going to run Alisha's plates, see if I can find her car."

"Have the Sioux City police check down by the bus station, John. I think that's where she dumped it, I say."

CHAPTER THIRTY-THREE

A quiet night, I am reading T. S.'s poem about men and the way they see themselves. Sheriff John has a better library than I would have thought. I believe everyman has a Prufrock within him. I do not want to be disturbed, I want to think about Michelangelo and scuttling claws. The doorbell rings. I wait. If John is home he will answer it. If not, maybe whoever it is will go away. I know I am brave enough to eat a peach. Ahh the Mermaids. Never to be forgotten. The doorbell rings again.

Okay, dammit anyway, here I come.

I never look through a peephole. I was warned by someone that a bullet fired into a peephole follows the path of least resistance through the door, into the looker's eye, and then through the back of their brain. Maybe that is true, maybe hokum. But I still am not looking into that peephole.

Who can it be? Probably not friendly, no one is that friendly to me. Could be Frank except he would probably call, not visit. Sheriff John is probably still on patrol, since he's not answering it. He wouldn't have rung the doorbell anyway.

I make sure the door is locked and the bolt pulled. I have no firearms, so I strap my knife on my right ankle and crawl out the window of my bedroom. I see no one to either side. There are street lights on both corners and in front of the house. An overhead light is also lit at mid-block back down in the alley, right behind John's garage. I hear the doorbell ring again. Then I hear a loud knock, then a kick, another kick and the door slams against something and I hear glass shattering.

I draw my knife and crouch to the side of the window. I hear stomping and cursing. Things are breaking, doors are slamming and presto, a head sticks out of my window. Brode. I slash his face with the knife and his head goes back into the house. I know I cut him pretty deep. I retreat across the neighbor's lawn to the rear of his house and go around the corner to where I can see the far side of the next house. Two shots come out the window, then I hear him crawling through the window. I walk as fast as I can up to look across the road. There is no one visible. I can see the motorcycle parked in front of John's house. I walk toward the street as fast as I can, cross it and go up the space between two houses heading for a back yard. I am trying to be quiet and put distance between Brode's pistol and me.

Visibility is reduced and I walk into a wire clothes line. It hits me in the mouth and whips my head backward. I almost fall but regain my balance. I walk toward the alley where, on this block, there is no light. I know I cannot remain hidden for long. Brode is faster and stronger than me. He probably has eyes out looking for me also. I am worried about Thatcher now also as Brode would not be brave enough to rush the Sheriff's house unless he knew the sheriff was not there and in too much trouble to return soon.

I walk at least twenty-five to thirty yards as fast as I can, crossing the street. I know I severely cut Brode. He is bleeding. Hopefully his vision is impaired. I walk another ten yards toward the back of the house when I hear gunfire behind me and the crisp zippy sound of a round goes past. I walk as close as I can to the side of one of the houses. Turn a corner and hear another round smash into the house slightly above where my head had been.

I go into a back yard. Much darker here and I am out of the direct line of fire. I am surprised at how much faster I can walk when I heard that gunfire. Brode is crossing the street now. I bump into a chain link fence. I start to roll over it, change my mind and stand on it instead. It is fastened to the side of a garage. I hold onto the roof of the garage, brace myself against a tree growing there, and jump up high enough on the roof that the weight of my body holds me up. I roll my feet up over the lip of the roof. The roof is slanted down at both the sides and in the rear. I roll onto the rear portion of the roof and lay as quiet as I can, knowing I am pretty well hidden by the dark, the branches of the tree, and the roof. My heart is thundering and I am breathing heavily but I control that as much as I can. If I can't see him maybe he will not see me. As a former hunter, I know that both the pursued and the searcher seldom look up. I flatten myself against the tiles remaining as motionless as possible. The hunter's eye can pick up the motion of a black object even in the darkest night. He stumbles over something in the back yard, curses, and keeps coming. The gate for the fence opens, making a scraping sound. I can see him now. He is holding a pistol in front of him, slowly turning his head, he is looking up and then down the alley.

After what seems hours, he walks to the right, following the alley as it moves toward the lights of town. When I see that he has moved more than half way down toward the corner, I roll back to the side of the garage, grasp a tree branch, and I swing my feet off the edge of the roof easing myself onto the fence. I sit on the fence and finally jump off. Ground feels good. I walk back to Thatcher's house. I go through the kitchen picking up a chef's knife as I walk, then on out to the garage. I need a better weapon. I find a hammer and a small hatchet on John's work bench. There are two full rolls of duct tape on his work bench. I unscrew the bristle end from his push broom, lift the handle, by itself. It has a nice heft and feel. I tape the chef's knife to one end of the handle. It makes a rudimentary pike, a weapon that I can use at a distance. Now if I could just find a shield to protect me from his gun. I bring the hammer and hatchet along. Turning off the lights, I return to the house.

I smile to myself. Brode has spent his life as the aggressor. He will never believe an old geezer will be hunting him. That is the one advantage I have. He has the arrogance of youth and strength, I have cunning and experience.

I walk through the house turning off the lights and walk out the front door. I cannot see him. I punch a hole in his gas tank with the hatchet and throw a kitchen match into the stream of gasoline. Fire lights up the street. I go back into the house. One or two minutes later, the bike explodes. The neighborhood rocks. People come out from almost every house, see the bike burning, and go back inside quickly. Not something they want to get involved in.

I can see Brode now. I am standing inside the house in the shadows, looking out through the front window. He is watching his bike burn. Blood is running down the left side of his face onto his jacket. Now he looks back across the street, then down the street, away from town. He starts to walk to the house. He has figured it out or it's a lucky guess. Probably a good guess for the dummy. Since the house is dark and he has been watching the fire, I am sure he cannot see me standing just inside the door. He is about five feet from entering the open front door when I throw the hatchet at him. It hits him mid-body and the hatchet bounces off, but he

steps back from the force of the blow before rushing forward. He raises his pistol and fires at the open doorway. I feel a burn along the left side of my chest. I throw the hammer just as hard and it slams into his body. I slam the door as hard as I can, twist and pick up the broom handle with the chef's knife. He kicks the door open violently. I throw my spear as hard as I can as soon as I see the door begin to move. The timing is perfect and the blade of my rudimentary spear just clears the edge of the door on its way to entering his throat with the full force of the throw backed by the weight of the handle. He pulls the trigger on his pistol twice. I hear it click, click, as the hammer falls on empty cylinders. He falls over backward from the force of the spear.

I turn on the lights. He has pulled out the knife and is trying to stem the blood loss with his hands. The pistol is lying on the ground where he dropped it. He is still standing, watching me. His hatred should be enough to roast me where I stand.

"Brode," I say, "Nice to meet you finally. That knife that was in your throat, that is for Jennie. I wasn't sure anyone else would avenge her, so I wanted to. I think we are even on that score. Just tell me if you think we are not even on Jennie."

He is lying on his back, motionless and holding his throat. I am not going near his legs. I have made the mistake before of coming too close to a wounded opponent. I thought he would be tougher than this.

I pick up the telephone and call 911.

"I have killed an intruder who was breaking into Sheriff Thatcher's house." I say and hang up.

His eyes follow me as I go to where he dropped his pistol.

I take his pistol and stick it in my waist band. I wipe down the hatchet, the broom handle and the chef's knife. I realize I cannot clean everything, but as a matter of course I can have some fingerprints here being John's house guest. I put the hammer down my waist band next to the pistol. I need to tighten my belt to hold my pants up.

I watch Brode try to adjust his grip on his throat so he can breathe easier. He has stopped the blood from flowing. By turning on his side, he has opened an airway. I pick up my pike and bury the knife end deep into his lower abdomen. He is not going to survive this night. All I need is a mean ugly asshole filled with hatred like Brode following me.

The sirens are getting louder. I see blue and red flashing light. I walk out the back door, go into the garage and peel off a twelve inch piece of duct tape. I lift my shirt and put the tape over the wound on my left side opened up by Brode's last bullet. It had entered my side at about elbow height, bounced off a rib and exited again. There are two distinct holes eight inches apart.

I make my way to the northwestern corner of town and carefully approach Brode's house. I can see no lights and hear nothing going on inside the house. I bang on the door. No answer. I go in the front door, walk directly to the kitchen table, slide it aside and move the linoleum. I lift the trapdoor and go down. Walk to the freezer, and smash the padlock with the hammer. Within a minute of beating on the lock, it falls apart.

I remove it and the chain. Open the freezer. I am violently ill by what I see. I am able to just move my head far enough to keep the vomit from going onto the bodies. I remove the top body and place her on the pallet. I look long and hard at the second body. My emotions almost overcome me. I have to keep my senses about me to get through this.

I close the freezer. Leave the hammer there. I take the rest of the money blocks in a plastic bag and climb the ladder out of the basement. I put nothing back, just leave out the front. I walk all the way out of town and walk the six miles out to Kelley's farm. I am worried that my stash has been found. It's safe and is all there. I pull out all my gear, take my meds, find a cigar, walk out on the porch roof and sit and puff.

I call Sheriff Thatcher. "Sorry I left your house in a mess, John. Your town will be cleaned out now. There is a person who needs your help in the basement of Brode's house. You should go right away and take an ambulance."

I know there are absolute rules for search warrants. I could report the drugs in his basement and the bodies in his basement, but he would never get a search warrant on allegations. But he can go anywhere if he reasonably expects to help save someone. He will find the bodies and arrest the rest of the gang. The town will be behind him when they see the horror of the freezer.

EPILOGUE

I have my backpack ready to go by early morning. I pack my camping gear and tent. I will have to leave some camping stuff, but I can get my fishing gear in. Everything else fits in including the Glock which I still have. I have tossed away all my clothes as I will not need more for a while. It's six in the morning and I am standing on highway 60 hitching east when Frank pulls up for me.

"Where you headed?"

"Sioux City, always wanted to see it," I say.

"Well get in then, I'm headed there also. Like the new car?"

"I do. Insurance come already?"

"Nope, I just went and bought it. Figured you would be leaving and I felt we should have wheels. I am off for the next two weeks so I'm hoping you won't mind a little company."

He pulls into the Cowboy's Restaurant in Yankton. "Let's have breakfast."

We both order coffee and eggs. Sit there looking at each other.

"Frank, I don't really know where I am going and I won't be good company. I have to find Alisha. I suspect the bartender, Al, will be with her. When I find her and Al, I will kill them both. I want you to understand that. There will be no bringing in the law and there won't be any mercy."

"Yep, that's what I figured. Do you have any place you think we should start?"

"Yes. If you are determined to come along, let's finish here, get an Atlas, and drive down by the dam. I will explain what I think there."

"Think we are going to find her in Illinois. I found out from the hit man that her name was actually Janet Sudacao. She and her husband had been involved with the Syndicate. I know it was in Southern Illinois. Something happened to cause them to move. I suspect they turned informant and were relocated to South Dakota under witness protection.

Therefore, I think, she is living with Al and Chris, the bartender from Avalon. I also, think the town is in Illinois, south of I-90 and north of Mount Vernon. She will probably pick a town with a population between fifty thousand and one hundred thousand. Big enough to have the amenities, small enough not to have the Syndicate. I think Al will want a college town because he wants to open a jumping bar with swarms of younger women.

One more thing, Frank, she has a big thing for Marines. She will want to live near a Marine Corps Facility or Camp. I don't know of any in Illinois but we should check."

We drive through to Iowa City when I ask him to stop for the night. As we check in to the motel, I ask the desk girl where the nearest hospital is.

The nurse at the emergency desk is just a little bulldoggish. "I am on Medicare I tell her. My Social Security number is 123-45-6789. Here is my passport for proof of identity."

"I need your Medicare card and your driver's license," she snaps.

"My billfold with my driver's license and Medicare card was stolen. I have requested a duplicate. I was shot earlier and I don't think I can wait for the duplicates to come in."

"Well," she snorts, "I have to check. Please be seated for a moment. I think I can find it on the computer, grumble, grumble, my supervisor check, grumble, grumble. Where did you get shot? No, I mean physically like on a map where, grumble, grumble, I need to contact the police you know. It's the law. More forms to fill out. Grumble, grumble. Your age?"

Finally, I do see a doctor who cleans and dresses my side. X-rays reveal a broken rib so I get a lot of tape. The police come and admonish Frank for not checking his firearm before cleaning it. The paperwork finally done, bill paid with Frank's credit card, and we are free to leave. As we walk by the Head Nurse, who is still grumbling and stomping around, we both smile, thank her for being so helpful and wish her a great evening. Frank had loaned me his gun, I can end all her unhappiness right now.

In the morning, we drive over to Monmouth, Ill., the closest town to meet our search parameters. We spend the afternoon watching two of the larger supermarkets in town. By six o'clock we call it and go for dinner. We spend time that evening going through the nightclubs, bars and hot spots. We see nothing of Al, Chris, or Alisha.

When we get back to the motel, Frank says, "I think I got the Marine connection. The football team at Western Illinois University is called 'The Leathernecks." That town is just south of here, Macomb."

We check into the Holiday Inn in Macomb, the next morning. Same plan as before. Frank drops me off at a large supermarket and he finds another. We had discussed looking through recent house and bar sales and that might be the way we have to go, but we will try the supermarkets first. We figure even those snakes have to eat.

I walk the aisles for several hours and then sit at their lunch bar/restaurant for a cup of coffee. I still am keeping an eye out for the lady with the pretty hair. I am sure her name is no longer Alisha. A tall blond man, weighing about two hundred and fifty pounds and wearing casual clothes, slides in across from me.

"Excuse me, sir," he says, "may I talk to you for a minute?"

"Sure Chris. It is Chris isn't it?"

"Yes, I'm Chris. Here's the thing. I knew you would be coming and I wanted to let you know that I am only a bartender. I was the bartender in Avalon, also. But that was all I did. I never sold drugs, or collected money for the girls or anything. I came out here to Macomb because my cousin, Al, said he had a job for me at his bar. I don't even work for him. I got a different job where I just serve beer in plastic cups. They like me because of my size. I didn't know all that stuff was going on until I rode out with Al. His name is Bob, now. So if you came to take me to the police, I will go with you."

What's the name of Bob's new bar?"

"It's the 'Good Mood bar.'"

"What did they change their name to?"

"He is Robert Keefer and she is Maxine Keefer. They live over at Lamoine Village, number 116. They bought a house but are having work done on it and won't get in for at least two months. I don't even live with them. I really wish I could have found another job back in Avalon. My new job is pretty nice though and I get good tips.

"I will leave you alone, Chris. Congratulations on your new job and life. Don't tell Bob and Maxine that you saw me, okay?

"I promise, I won't."

I call Frank.

Frank and I have a long night. We need a bottle of Scotch and six cigars. He finally agrees with me, at least, he will wait to see. I take a card out of Green Hat's wallet and make a call.

Frank and I go to Chicago the next day. We schedule in a Bull's game that evening. Cold beer and great basketball. Hooray, they win. Later that same evening, sitting in our hotel room, we see a report on WGN TV about a mob hit on two people in Lamoine Village, Macomb, Ill. The reporter is outraged. Not so much outrage for Frank and me.

I am on my way in a taxi down to the Amtrak station at 600 West La Salle. It's six in the morning. Frank is still sleeping. I leave most of the money on my bed for him. I have a couple of bricks and a ticket for Seattle. I will need my fly rod in Seattle.

ABOUT THE AUTHOR

David is a former U.S. Navy Corpsman who spent time attached to the Marine Corps. He earned a Bachelor's degree from Northwestern College and Master's degree from Western Illinois University. He currently resides in Port St. Lucie, Florida, with his wife and three dogs.

WEBSITE: http://www.tienterd.com/author/
FACEBOOK: https://www.facebook.com/Dave.Tienter

www.ingramcontent.com/pod-product-compliance
Lightning Source LLC
Chambersburg PA
CBHW070750280626
47162CB00018B/2878